"Are you crying?" Kane asked.

She wasn't a crier. She'd never been a crier. Even when she'd discovered the truth about Randy, she hadn't cried. She certainly wasn't going to cry now. She sniffed again, trying to prove that truth to herself.

"Why would I be?" she asked, not opening her eyes because she was afraid a tear might slip out.

"Because you've been running for weeks? Because you're tired? Because it's almost Christmas and you're far from home?"

Yes. To all those things.

"I'm this close to decrypting that file, Kane. I just want to get somewhere where I can concentrate on doing it," she responded.

He didn't say anything. Just let the truck fill with their silences.

That was fine.

She was fine.

Or, she would be.

Once she fulfilled her promise to Juniper and made it back home.

Please, God, let that happen. Please, she prayed silently, her eyes still closed as the truck descended the mountain.

Mary Ellen Porter's love of storytelling was solidified in fifth grade when she was selected to read her first children's story to a group of kindergartners. From then on, she knew she'd be a writer. When not working, Mary Ellen enjoys reading and spending time with her family and search-dog-in-training. She's a member of Chesapeake Search Dogs, a volunteer search and rescue team that helps bring the lost and missing home.

Books by Mary Ellen Porter

Love Inspired Suspense

Into Thin Air
Off the Grid Christmas

OFF THE GRID CHRISTMAS

MARY ELLEN PORTER

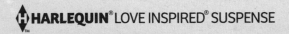

HARLEQUIN® LOVE INSPIRED® SUSPENSE

Recycling programs
for this product may
not exist in your area.

LOVE INSPIRED BOOKS

ISBN-13: 978-0-373-67856-3

Off the Grid Christmas

www.Harlequin.com

I am the Lord. I am the God of every person on the earth. You know that nothing is impossible for Me.
–Jeremiah 32:27

To my parents, Ed and Shirley Porter,
whose constant love and encouragement have
guided all my life choices and underpinned my successes.
Thank you for your unfailing support and for giving me
a strong foundation of faith and family.

And to my in-laws, Eldridge and Joyce Grady, for
embracing me as your own from the first day we met.
I couldn't have asked for a more perfect extended family.

ONE

The Christmas tree had been Arden DeMarco's undoing.

Or, to be more accurate, the decorations on it had.

Not that accuracy mattered. What mattered was that she had to leave. Quickly.

She shoved her sweatshirt into her backpack, the scent of Tide detergent and lavender fabric softener reminding her of her childhood home. She'd hoped to be there for Christmas, reveling in the beautiful predictability of Christmas Eve service, ham dinner, new pajamas worn on Christmas morning.

She was twenty-five years old and she still loved those things.

Unfortunately, in this instance her nostalgia had been her downfall.

She sighed.

What was done was done. For twelve days she'd been safe in this secluded cottage just outside of Lubec, Maine. Now she wasn't.

She hadn't planned to leave, but staying was

no longer an option. She'd have to find another place to go to ground. With a quick look around the room, Arden was satisfied she was leaving nothing important behind. No clues as to what she'd been working on, where she planned to go or what her next step would be.

Zipping her pack, she gave the surveillance monitors one more glance.

All clear.

For now. But the odds weren't in her favor.

Grabbing the wearable pet carrier from the hook behind the door that separated the kitchen from the cozy living room, she fastened it around her chest.

"Sebastian? Time to go," she called.

As was Sebastian's way, he didn't answer.

She crossed the room to check his favorite spot, knelt down and peered under the sparsely decorated Christmas tree. Sure enough, he was there, batting at a red bulb.

"Did you learn nothing from the tinsel incident?" she muttered.

He looked at her, blinking large blue eyes and meowing as she scooped him up and placed him in the carrier. Where most cats would have yowled and struggled, he settled in without a fuss, the tips of his dark brown ears barely visible as she pulled the drawstring on the carrier to secure him inside. Like Arden, he was quirky. It was one of the reasons she'd adopted him.

He purred happily against her chest. Poor guy had no idea that he'd brought danger down on their heads.

She'd been so careful when she'd dropped off the grid. Covered all the bases: cash transactions only, no contact with family, prepaid cell phone for emergencies only. There'd been no way anyone could trace her movements.

Or so she'd thought.

Unfortunately, in her panic, she'd forgotten about Sebastian's microchip. Truth be told, if Sebastian hadn't eaten his body weight in tinsel, she'd still be none the wiser. Okay. It hadn't been that much tinsel. After administering an ultrasound, the vet had assured Arden that the cat would be just fine. She'd been happy and relieved until the vet had called an hour ago to check on Sebastian and used Arden's real name.

A name Arden hadn't used in almost two weeks. They'd obviously scanned Sebastian for a microchip and now her assumed alias and the cottage address were linked to Arden's true identity, through the PetID database.

The jig was up. She needed to leave. If she managed to escape with her life, she'd never *ever* hang tinsel again.

A powerful gust of wind whipped in from the ocean, drawing her attention to the window. The sun had set an hour ago, and the full moon should have been rising above the ocean.

Clouds covered it, light gray against the dark horizon. Below, the beach lay empty. No lights or bonfires. No people with flashlights digging for clams. This wasn't the time of year for vacationers. That had played to Arden's advantage. Now she felt vulnerable.

She tried to tell herself it was good that she was leaving, but she'd wanted to stay. A quiet cottage far away from anyone who knew her had been the perfect place to hide.

The wind buffeted the cottage's shake siding and howled beneath the eaves, the eerie sound spurring her to hurry. She pulled on her coat, partially zipping it up over Sebastian. He purred even more loudly.

Happy cat.

Unhappy human companion.

Arden shoved gloves into her pockets and yanked a knit cap over her ears. This was it. Time to go. She grabbed her pack, flipped off the lights and dropped the house keys on the desk next to a note about the security system she'd regrettably be leaving behind. State-of-the-art. Expensive. She'd probably need it again before this was over, but it was too heavy and cumbersome for someone who needed to move quickly.

The perimeter alarm chirped, the warning sending her pulse racing. She turned back to the monitors. Three were clear. The fourth showed a lone figure making his way slowly up the steep snow-covered path on foot. She smiled at that. She'd chosen this location well—even a Jeep couldn't navigate the narrow, rock-covered road.

One guy she could handle.

She had the advantage. She knew he was coming.

The cottage was in a large clearing, no place to conceal movement—perfect for seeing what was coming; not so great for a covert escape.

She'd wait until he was on the front walkway, then sneak out the back.

She shrugged the pack onto her shoulders, her attention on the monitor as the man strode up the walkway.

Keeping an eye on the monitor, she crossed the well-worn wood floor to the back door. Heart pounding, hand on the doorknob, she waited for him to reach the front steps. A cold breeze swept in under the door and she shivered. The 1930s cottage, mostly used as a summer rental, was not well insulated. Though it was comfortable enough with both wood-burning stoves fired up, she had extinguished the fires thirty minutes ago in preparation for her departure. Now, with the embers quickly cooling, the cold Maine chill was settling over the house.

The man reached the front steps, eyed the footprints she'd left in the snow when she'd returned from the vet. The image on the monitor wasn't clear enough to see his face, but she didn't plan to stick around long enough to get a better look.

"Get ready for a bumpy ride, Sebastian," Arden muttered, quietly opening the back door. The new storm door stuck, the old frame a poor fit. She should have removed it when she'd first noticed the problem, but she hadn't thought she'd be found. Assumptions could get a person killed. Her oldest brother and decorated FBI agent, Grayson, was always saying that. Hopefully, she wasn't going to prove him right.

She walked outside, letting the door rest against the jamb. No time to wrestle it tightly into place. The yard was a slick sheet of icy snow, but she rushed toward the back corner of the property as quickly as she could. She had to reach the shed, and the motorcycle, if she had any hope of escape. She had minutes. Maybe less.

Bang!

The sound sent adrenaline coursing through her blood.

She glanced back, saw the storm door lifted by the wind.

Bang!

The door slammed again, and a dark figure appeared around the corner of the house. Tall. Obviously masculine. Coming toward her with quick, decisive steps.

She sprinted to the shed.

"Arden DeMarco!" the man yelled, his voice carrying over the sound of the crashing surf and wind.

She reached for the shed door with shaking hands, yanked it open just as he grabbed her shoulder.

Arden was ready for him.

The youngest of five children, and the only girl, she'd learned to hold her own early on—her brothers had made sure of that. And what they hadn't taught her, ten years of mixed martial arts training had. Without hesitation, she pivoted, grabbing his hand and twisting it at an unnatural angle.

He released his hold, giving her just enough space to throw a punch. He dodged at the last minute, her knuckles just brushing his jaw. She pulled back, aiming for his throat this time. She'd practiced this move dozens of times. She knew it cold, but Sebastian hindered her movement and the man was quicker than she expected, grabbing her wrist and yanking her arm down before she could land the blow.

"Enough!" he growled. "I'm just here to—"

She threw a left hook. Her fist connected.

She knew what he was there for. Or she could guess. He was too well trained to be anything but a government operative or a hired assassin.

If he felt the blow at all, he didn't let on. Instead, he raised his arm to block her next punch.

"I said, enough," he muttered, his foot sweeping

out, catching her ankle as she dodged. She stumbled backward, managed to somehow regain her balance. He reached for her again, grabbing the sleeve of her jacket and pulling her toward him.

Arden was small, agile and packed a surprising punch for her size. But Kane Walker had spent more than ten years in the Special Forces as part of the army's elite Night Stalkers airborne brigade, and she was no match for him.

Not that he planned to keep fighting her.

He'd come to bring her home.

She was going. Whether she liked it or not.

"Arden, your—" he began, but she was obviously in no mood to listen.

She yanked away, took a stance he'd seen dozens of times when he'd sparred with her brother Jace. She attacked with Jace's signature move. It was almost indefensible.

Almost.

He took a calculated step forward, got his knee behind her leg and swept her toward the ground. If she'd been an enemy, he would have added a punch to the chest or nose to speed her descent; instead, he grabbed her arm as she flew backward, slowing her fall. She hit the ground with a thud anyway.

"How about we call a truce?" he said, holding his hands up in mock surrender. "Jace didn't have me track you down so we could spar."

"Jace?" She got to her feet, eyeing him through the darkness. He doubted she could see his features in the unlit yard. Even if she could, she might not be able to place his face. They'd met a few times in the past. Mostly when he'd joined Jace on home leave.

"Your brother's worried about you."

"And you know this because?" she asked, her shoulders tense, her hands fisted.

"I'm Kane Walker. Your brother's—"

"Business partner," she finished.

"Right."

"So, Kane," she said, sidling along the shed she was backed against. Unless he missed his guess, there was another door in and she was going for it. "Why'd Jace send you when he could have sent any one of my brothers?"

"You've hit the FBI's most wanted list."

"I'm aware of that."

"The Feds are watching your entire family. Since you and I are barely acquaintances, I'm not on their radar."

"Yet."

"Yet," he agreed as she shimmied to the corner of the shed, pivoted and took off.

He snagged her pack, yanking her backward with enough force to throw her off balance. "I thought we were done sparring, Arden."

"You need to leave." She spun around.

"Not without you."

"Let me make this perfectly clear: I'm not going anywhere with you. Make this easy on yourself. Go back to Maryland. And tell my brothers that I'm fine."

"Jace told me to bring you to Grayson—you can deal with the FBI together."

"Jace is going to be very disappointed." She crossed her arms over her chest.

Actually, she crossed them over her bulging stomach. He frowned, eyeing the mound under her coat. It wiggled.

"Carrying a passenger?"

"My cat."

"Might have been a good idea to leave him home. Microchips can make it difficult to drop completely off the grid."

"I'm aware of that," she said.

"Yet you brought him to the vet anyway," he pointed out.

"I was worried," she said defensively, her left hand reaching up to cradle the mound under her jacket. "Though it really was an unfortunate turn of events that the Lubec Veterinary Clinic uses microchip scanners."

"I guess that depends on your point of view." For Kane, it was just the break he'd been waiting for.

She stepped past him, acting like she was going to go ahead and do what she'd been trying to since he'd arrived—leave.

"I hope you're not thinking that you're going anywhere without me."

"I'm not thinking it. I'm doing it."

After nearly six days without a lead, he'd arrived in this snowy ocean-side town under no delusion that getting her home would be simple. She knew how to hide, and she knew how to fight. According to Jace, she also had a tendency to be dogmatic in her approach to things and often unwilling to compromise.

"I'm afraid you've misunderstood. I'm bringing you home, so we're going to have to stick together from here on out."

"Sorry, that doesn't work for me. I prefer solitude to company," she said, tugging open the door to the shed.

He pushed it shut again. "I prefer cooperation to animosity, but we don't always get what we want."

"You're in my personal space," she responded, ignoring his comment. "How about you get out of it?"

He stepped closer, tired of the wordplay and anxious to get her away from the property. "Now you're in mine."

"Personal space is the variable and subjective distance at which one person feels comfortable talking to another. If you want to speak with me, you need to back away."

He almost cracked a smile. Almost.

She wasn't looking for a chat. She was looking

for an escape route. He could see it in her eyes. Her body language.

She was Jace's sister through and through. If the black hair and blue eyes weren't a dead give-away, the stubborn set of her jaw certainly was.

"Let's take the FBI out of the picture for a minute. What are you running from?" he asked, his right hand still holding the shed door closed. His arm just above her shoulder blocked escape from her left.

"Trouble," she replied, glancing to her right as if calculating the likelihood of dodging out of his reach.

"Better to face it with a support system than alone."

"I can't involve anyone else. It's too dangerous."

"You can explain that to your brother when you see him."

"Returning to Maryland isn't an option."

Kane shook his head. "From where I stand, it's the only option."

"Well, if you'd just back up about a foot and take a few steps to your left, *my* preferred option will become a little clearer to you."

He could have laughed if he'd let himself. Jace had said his sister was brilliant. He hadn't mentioned her sense of humor.

"Sorry. That's not going to happen. I promised Jace that I'd find you and bring you home."

"You should never make a promise you can't

keep." Her back against the door, she slowly edged her way toward the right corner of the shed.

He grabbed her left arm just below the elbow, and stopped her in her tracks. "We're wasting time," he said. "I found you—it's safe to assume someone else will, too. If you don't want to tell me why you're running, maybe you can tell me who you're running from."

"I'm running from so many people, it would almost be easier to tell you who isn't after me." She tucked a few strands of hair under her hat, her gaze shifting from him to a point beyond his shoulder.

"Go ahead."

"And leave? I was thinking about it, but it's hard to do with you holding onto my arm."

"Go ahead and list the people who aren't after you."

She sighed, tried to yank her wrist away. "Look, I know you're trying to do what Jace wants, but I can handle this alone. I won't drag him, Grayson or even you into this."

"We're already in it," he pointed out, and she frowned.

"You don't have to be. You can walk away and let me go back to what I was doing."

He was tempted to do just that.

He didn't have time for games. After twelve years of active duty, he'd left the army in August and spent the last three months getting his and Jace's fledgling business off the ground.

Shadow Wolves Security, named after their Army unit, was finally up and running. It had taken a lot of work. With Jace's tour not up for another four months, the bulk of it had fallen on Kane. He'd spent countless unpaid hours making certain things were ready. He'd even managed to land their first contracts, set to start in less than a month.

With that under his belt, he'd planned to leave the business in the hands of his other business partner and Chief Operations Officer, Silas Blackwater, and take a long, relaxing weekend. Jace's phone call had changed his plans. When he'd asked Kane to help Grayson locate their sister, Kane couldn't refuse.

Yeah. He might be tempted to walk away and let Arden deal with her problem alone, but he wouldn't do it. He owed Jace a lot. More than he could ever repay.

"Let's go." He still had his hand around her wrist, and he started walking, dragging her along beside him, not caring that she was yanking against his hold.

"You don't understand the ramifications of me going back," she muttered, digging in her heels and putting all her weight into trying to stop their forward momentum. There wasn't a whole lot of weight to her, so it barely slowed Kane down.

"Explain it to me then."

"The people who are after me are dangerous and they've got deep pockets. They'll stop at nothing to get what they want. They don't care who they hurt in the process."

"Grayson can work with the FBI to clear your name and protect you."

"I trust Grayson, but I can't ask him to put his career on the line and take my side against the FBI. Besides, there's no way to be sure they don't have someone in the FBI on their payroll."

"Who, exactly, are *these people*, and what do they want from you?"

"That information is need-to-know." She tucked another loose strand of hair beneath her hat. A nervous tic? he wondered.

"I need to know."

"You are an intermediary. You only need to know that I'm not returning home. Not yet. Tell my brothers—"

A loud chirp interrupted her words. Two more followed in rapid succession.

He didn't ask what it was.

He knew.

She'd set up a perimeter alarm and it was going off.

"What quadrant?" he asked as she pulled a cell phone from her coat pocket.

"West. Looks like the same way you arrived. You'd better go—"

The phone chirped again.

"Sounds like they have an army coming for you." He sprinted back to the shed, pulling her along with him. She'd been trying to get inside since he'd arrived.

Now, she seemed determined *not* to enter.

She tried to twist away, but his fingers easily locked around her slender wrist. He dragged her into the shed, easing the door closed and sealing them inside. It smelled like sawdust and gas fumes.

"You have a vehicle in here?" he asked, keeping his grip on her wrist tight. He didn't want to hurt her, but he wasn't going to let her leave. Not on her own.

"That would be a likely scenario, since I've been trying to get in here since you arrived," she grumbled, jerking away and moving toward the center of the shed.

"How about you show it to me so we can get moving?" he demanded, his gaze shifting to a lone window that looked out over the beach. It was too dark to see much, but a light bounced along the shore. He doubted it was a beachcomber looking for treasures.

"It's under the tarp," she responded, motioning to the center of the room.

"Then let's go." He crowded in beside her, blocking her path to the door. She had her reasons for continuing to run. He had his reasons for bringing her home. They could hash all that out, come up with a plan that would work for both of them. Later.

After they escaped whomever it was she was running from.

TWO

Someone had breached her security perimeter.

Someone else was on the beach.

Through the shed window, Arden could see the light moving along the shore—a small dot of white in the blackness. She doubted it was just one person. And she doubted it was the FBI.

Grayson probably told Kane to monitor the PetID database for a potential hit on Sebastian's microchip, but there's no way her brother would have shared that information with the FBI.

Arden's ex-boyfriend Randy Sumner was another story.

He knew about Sebastian, and he'd have no qualms about tipping off GeoArray Corporation. He was in this deep and had just as much to lose if the company went down. And he, more than anyone, knew Arden could bring them all down.

She hadn't been exaggerating about GeoArray's power, resources and reach. The corporation *was* an army of sorts, and it would send its best soldiers to bring her in.

Soldiers? Thugs was probably a more accurate

descriptor, and unless Arden missed her guess, they were trying to hem her in.

But she'd be gone before whoever was on the beach managed to make it up the bluff. Kane would be with her. She wasn't happy about it. It would be easier to leave him behind, but he had no idea what Arden was up against; what *he* was now up against.

Arden knew. They'd killed before. They wouldn't hesitate to kill again. No, she couldn't, in good conscience, leave Kane to face off against them.

Sure, he was former Special Forces and looked like he could take care of himself. She'd seen him sparring with her brothers at the gym while he and Jace were on home leave one summer. She knew he was quick, sharp-minded and lethal, but Geo-Array had money and power behind it. So did its CEO, Marcus Emory. They wouldn't fight fair and could afford to hire the best fighters and trackers to hunt down what they wanted.

At this moment, what they wanted was Arden.

They were desperate to get their hands on her and the files she'd taken from their networks.

She'd given them a golden opportunity, thanks to her love for Christmas and Sebastian. Now, she had to get out of their reach, and she needed to get Kane out, too.

She dragged the canvas tarp off the motorbike her landlord had left in the shed. A 1952 Vincent

Black Shadow. Admittedly, the bike had seen better days. But Arden appreciated the handcraftsmanship of the vehicle and the fact that, in its heyday, the model broke speed records. Very few had been made.

Arden suspected the property owner had no idea of the value the bike would bring if restored. If he did, he might not be so quick to leave it in an unlocked shed for his renters to use.

"A motorcycle?" Kane pressed close to her back, in her space again. Usually, she despised having people that close. Currently, she didn't have time to worry about it or to tell him to back off.

"Does it look like something else?"

"It looks old."

"It is."

"Does it work?"

"Yep. It came with the rental—it's a way residents can get up and down the access path to the parking area more quickly."

"I'm afraid to ask how loud it's going to be when you start it up." He glanced toward the window. "There's someone out on the beach. I can't tell if he's alone."

"It's too far down with no easy way up. Anyone on the beach shouldn't pose much of a threat. The bigger threat is whoever's coming up the access path. The shed's in clear view of it. Once we're in the open, we'd be easily picked off by anyone with a high-powered rifle."

"What are you suggesting?"

She turned her attention back to her phone, scrolled through the live video feed from her security system. "They've got no clue I know they're coming. Logic says they'll head for the house. As soon as it's breached, we can start her up and head for the trail at the back of the property. We'll be out of the line of fire before they can make it to the back door."

He glanced at the phone in her hand. "You've set up an elaborate monitoring system."

"Wouldn't you?"

"Yes, but I'm in the security business."

"I am, too. It's just a different kind of security."

Kane cracked open the shed door, his broad back blocking her view.

"See anything?" she asked. She'd have edged in closer, stuck her head under his arm to get a look, but Sebastian was getting restless. His fuzzy ears poked through the top flap of the carrier and bumped against her collarbone as he tried to figure out what was going on.

"Just a lot of darkness, but I don't like the way it feels."

"Darkness has a feeling?"

"Danger does." He grabbed the bike's handlebars, tugged the motorcycle forward and out of her grasp. "We need to move."

She could have argued, but she'd heard her brothers talk about going with their guts so many times, she didn't think it would be prudent to ignore Kane's instincts.

"The trail's kind of hidden. It's just behind the shed and winds toward the bigger path you walked in on." She leaned past, poked her head out the door and pointed at what looked like driftwood and scrappy bushes covered with a fresh layer of ice-crested snow. She wasn't sure if the owner of the property had meant to provide a quick escape, but she'd known as soon as she'd seen the narrow trail that she'd have one if she needed it.

She hadn't expected to need it.

Maybe that was part of her problem. She trusted in her intelligence a little too much. She relied on herself more than she relied on anyone else. She'd been one of the guys for as long as she could remember—the ultra-capable younger sister of four ultra-capable men. She'd never been in a situation she couldn't handle on her own, and she hadn't expected to find herself in one. She'd expected to go off the grid, get the proof she needed to take GeoArray down and go right back to her life. That wasn't how things were turning out.

She found that more irritating than alarming.

"You've ridden a motorcycle before, right?" she whispered, pocketing her phone as Kane pushed the vehicle outside, putting the shed between them and the access path to the cottage. The wind stole her words, but he must have heard.

"Not one this old," he responded.

"The age of the vehicle is irrelevant," she said, ignoring his sarcasm. She loved old vehicles and had restored several of them with her dad while helping out in his shop during the summers. She'd ridden this one enough to know it was in good working order. It was also fast. That was going to be an asset.

"Its working condition is *not* irrelevant."

"It works." They'd reached the brush, and she skirted past him. Not an easy feat considering his size, but there was no way she was letting him drive them out. She knew the trail. She knew the bike. She'd be the driver.

She brushed his hands from the handlebars and climbed on, balancing the bike as she scanned the dark path and the beach below. The light was still there. Farther away and moving at a steady pace, parallel to the shore. Whoever it was wouldn't find a way up from there, but night vision goggles and a long-range rifle could make a long-distance kill easy.

GeoArray wanted her alive. For now. That was one thing she had in her favor.

Kane, on the other hand, was simply in the way.

Her phone chirped, the sound chilling her blood.

"They're in," she muttered.

Kane climbed on the bike, wrapping his left arm low around her waist. "Just be careful," he warned. "The temperature's dropped and the snow's crusted over with ice. If we wreck, it's over."

"Warning duly noted." Arden zipped her jacket up to her chin, completely covering Sebastian. She didn't need Kane to tell her to be cautious. Wrecking the bike and getting herself caught was not on her agenda. Seeing her brother's business partner—one of his closest friends—killed wasn't, either.

She was sorry Kane had been dragged into this, but she wasn't surprised her brothers called for reinforcements. Grayson and Jace were cut from the same cloth, both willing to do anything to help those they cared about. It would be hypocritical to fault them for that. After all, that's how she ended up in this mess in the first place. Of course, Juniper Westin wasn't just anyone. She was Arden's best friend, the sister Arden had never had.

They'd met halfway through first grade. Juniper had walked into the classroom, and Arden had known they were kindred spirits—two oddball mavericks sitting in a room filled with average Joes.

The whispering had started right away, and Arden had felt the overwhelming need to stand up for the new girl the way she'd always had to stand up for herself. It wasn't Juniper's glasses or curly black hair that had all the kids talking; it wasn't her light brown skin—even though there hadn't been many kids of color in their elementary school.

No, it was the dark purple bruise on her cheek that accompanied the healing split on her lip. And the too-big sweater she'd had on with well-worn jeans that were almost too short. Jeans that had bright red patches with pink hearts carefully sewn on the knees. During recess, Robby Dixon had laughed at her for those hearts, and Arden had done the only thing she thought she could. She'd punched him right in the middle of his smug face. She'd earned herself a three-day suspension, the respect of every kid in the school and a life-long friend.

Since then, she and Juniper had been through good times and bad times together. There was nothing Arden wouldn't do for her friend—including hacking into GeoArray's secured network—which, unfortunately, had led to this.

Kane leaned in, his breath tickling her ear. "I just saw a light go on in the house. If we're getting out of here, now's the time to do it."

"Right." She cranked the engine, the sudden roar drowning out the sound of the surf. No doubt everyone within a mile radius had heard. She gunned the motor, and the bike charged forward, speeding through the narrow space between old shrubs, bits of leaves and branches breaking off as she raced along the trail.

To Kane's credit, he had no problem holding on and keeping his balance. He didn't shout instructions or tell her to watch out for the rocks and debris that littered the narrow trail.

And he'd been right about the ice. It coated everything. The bike's nearly threadbare tires barely held on as she sped around a curve.

She thought she heard shouting, but she couldn't be certain. The engine was too loud, the wind too wild. They'd be at the parking area soon. It was a small lot used by a few seasonal residents whose cliff-side cottages weren't easily accessible by car. It was mostly unused this time of year. Her Jeep was there. Kane's vehicle must be, too. She wasn't sure they'd be able to get to either of them. Geo-Array's thugs probably had the area staked out.

"Pull off here," Kane shouted.

She almost ignored him.

She wanted off the trail and on the open road. The more distance they put between themselves and their pursuers, the better. Then again, if guys with guns were waiting in the parking lot below, she'd have to drive straight into their trap before she could get out on the road.

She coasted to a stop and cut the engine, her pulse racing.

"Is there another way out?" Kane asked, his voice tight.

"We can head up the bluff." She nodded toward the south and the scraggly pines that dotted a steep hill. She'd walked there a couple of days ago, trying to clear her mind after hours in front of the computer. "But I don't know how far we can take the bike. The terrain's steep and icy and the bike's tires have definitely seen better days. We need a vehicle, and mine's in the lot."

"I parked off the street. About a half-mile from the lot."

A light flashed at the head of the trail, there and gone so quickly Arden would have missed it if she hadn't been looking in that direction.

"A signal," Kane muttered. "They're going to try to trap us. Can we make it to the road, or should we ditch the bike and try to make it out quietly? You know the area best. It's your call, Arden, but make the right choice. We're probably outmanned and outgunned."

"We can make it out on the bike." It would take a little finesse and a whole lot of guts, but their odds were better on the bike than walking out.

She started the engine and took off again, leaving the trail and bouncing onto ice-coated grass, speeding between spindly pine trees as she raced up the bluff and toward freedom.

Kane had been in a lot of dangerous situations, but riding on an ancient motorbike behind a woman who seemed more daredevil than computer whiz was right up at the top of his list of experiences he never wanted to repeat.

He was concerned about the icy conditions, Arden's driving skills and the fact that whoever was after her might have already spotted his rented Chevy Tahoe. It was unlikely, though. He'd parked behind a small copse of trees, and the vehicle would be difficult to spot from the road.

Still, if the people who were after Arden were as desperate as she seemed to believe, they might have been scoping out the area, looking for signs that someone besides Arden was around.

The bike bounced over an exposed root, and he tightened his grip on Arden's waist. He'd have preferred to drive, but this arrangement left his gun hand free. Arden navigated the rocky, snow-covered bluff with surprising ease.

Kane leaned forward, his chest pressing against Arden's backpack. The wind whipped at strands of hair peeking out from her hat, the soft tendrils brushing against his cheek.

She slowed as they reached the crest of the hill. Even at this speed the cold air was merciless on their exposed skin and eyes. They needed to get to the Chevy. He had a duffel of supplies there, hats and gloves, an extra jacket.

His work required preparedness, and he'd tried to think of all the possibilities when he'd set off to find Arden. He'd been hoping to be a few steps ahead of whoever was after her, but the army that was following her seemed to have a lot of tech power behind it—they'd been able to access the PetID database and register the hit on the microchip just as he had. They also had at least some knowledge of Arden's private life. Kane had only known about her cat and its microchip because Grayson had told him. Was it possible someone Arden knew well had set her up?

He glanced over his shoulder, his arm still tight around Arden's waist.

Bright lights illuminated the path they'd left, what looked like an ATV zipping along the narrow passage.

"They're coming. Looks like they have a vehicle that can make it," he warned.

"Hold on," she shouted, hitting the throttle and propelling them over the top of the bluff. The way down was as steep as the trip up, but the bike managed to cling to the rocky, ice-coated ground as Arden wove her way through sparse pine growth.

There weren't enough trees to provide adequate cover, and the hair on his neck stood on end. He may as well have had a bull's-eye on his back. One well-trained sniper, and he'd be down.

He glanced back. The ATV had crested the hill and seemed to be idling there. It was a good vantage point, and the shot would be easy enough to take.

Arden must have sensed the danger.

"Hang on!" she shouted. Hitting the throttle

once more, she increased their speed and veered sharply to the right, steering the motorcycle toward what looked like a shallow ditch. Beyond that, the road curved across the landscape.

The first shot rang out as the motorcycle jumped the ditch. Bits of bark flew into Kane's face as the tires hit the snowy pavement. The motorcycle wobbled dangerously, yet somehow remained upright.

"Left!" he shouted, calculating their distance from his Tahoe, the likelihood of the next bullet hitting its target, the chance that Arden would make it out of this situation alive if something happened to him.

He'd promised Jace he'd get her home in one piece.

He'd do it.

A second shot rang out, and the pavement behind them exploded. A high-caliber rifle, but the gunman couldn't seem to hit his mark.

There are always blessings in the trials.

His grandmother had reminded him of that dozens of times when he was a kid. Maybe she'd been right.

He could see the patch of trees where he'd parked the Tahoe, and the dull gleam of the street sign he'd used as a marker just ahead.

A bullet hit it, bouncing off the metal with a loud crack.

"Just past the sign. Behind those trees," he

barked, and Arden veered in the direction he'd indicated, the motorcycle slowing as she bounced off the road and into knee-high grass.

She cut the motor as they reached the Tahoe.

The night had gone silent except for the wind that howled through the trees. No engines roaring, people shouting, bullets flying.

"I don't like this," Arden whispered as she clambered off the bike.

"Get in!" he urged, opening the driver's side door. "They're probably coming from the parking area." Before the words were out of his mouth, she was scrambling across the bench seat; he rushed in after her, pulling the door shut behind him.

Shoving the keys in the ignition, Kane cranked the engine and hit the gas. The SUV lurched out from behind the trees and screeched onto the road.

"Keep down!" Kane ordered as he floored it.

He didn't know how many vehicles were coming from the parking area, but he could already see a set of lights in his rearview mirror. He might be able to outrun them.

Might.

He'd flown into a small airfield three miles away, just outside of Lubec. Bringing the Cessna had been faster and easier than driving or booking a commercial flight.

With the weather getting bad and the enemy on his tail, he wasn't sure it had been the right decision. The airfield shared space with Tommy's

Truck and SUV Rentals, the town's only car rental business; the pickings had been slim—mostly older model pickup trucks—and he'd thought he'd been fortunate enough to rent the Tahoe. Now he wished there'd been a faster vehicle to choose.

Arden shifted, and before he realized what she was doing, she was on her knees, peering out the back window.

"They're gaining on us," she commented.

There didn't seem to be any panic in her voice. So far, she'd been unflappable. That was good. Panic only ever caused people to make mistakes that could get them killed.

"Get out of your pack and get your seat belt on." He issued the order and ignored her comment.

"Are you expecting to crash?" But Arden shrugged out of her backpack and fastened the seat belt around her waist, carefully positioning the shoulder strap behind her so it wouldn't bother her cat.

"I'm expecting that they won't give up easily," he responded.

"Logic agrees."

"Does it?" he said drily as he sped around a curve in the road. The light disappeared from the rearview mirror. Gone for now, but not for long. If they hadn't been on a two-lane highway that overlooked a twenty-foot drop to the ocean, he'd have looked for a place to pull off and hide until their pursuers passed.

"Of course," Arden replied. "Now that they've used their weapons and shown their hand, they can't let us escape. They'll need to kill you to keep you from contacting the police once they've gotten their hands on me, so any way you cut it, they're not going to give up easily."

"Kill me, huh?"

"Does that surprise you?"

"No, but I'm curious."

"About?"

"Their reasons for wanting to take you alive."

"It's complicated."

"Yeah?" He glanced at the speedometer, its needle hovering around eighty-five. Any faster and the vehicle would start shaking like it was in need of a front-end alignment.

"Very." She answered absently, giving no further explanation.

"Care to tell me exactly *who* wants to keep you alive?"

"In actuality, there are several entities who might be responsible for this. I *am* on the FBI's most wanted list."

"You're avoiding my question."

"No. I'm just avoiding giving you an answer."

"Why?"

"My reasons are not your concern."

She obviously didn't trust him. He'd drop it. For now.

Arden twisted once more in her seat, looking out the back window. "Can this thing go any faster? I'm pretty sure I see headlights behind us again."

He could see them, too, but he'd already accelerated as much as the Tahoe could. "We've still got some distance between us."

"Not enough. Lubec's less than a mile away. If you avoid Main Street, we might be able to give them the slip."

"It's a small town, and there aren't many places to hide. I won't feel safe until we get you out of Lubec, and Maine altogether for that matter."

"That's unrealistic. If we can't beat them on this curved and twisting road, we can't beat them in a race on the open highway."

"You're assuming I'm planning to drive us out of here."

"Is there another option?" Her voice was sharp.

"I left my Cessna at the Coastal Airstrip just outside of town."

"Cessna?" she said a little too loudly, her voice tight. "*That's* your plan?"

"Yes."

"I don't fly," Arden stated firmly.

"You're about to." He took a sharp curve in the road. The turn into the airport access road was up ahead, and the headlights behind them had disappeared again. If he was fast enough, he could turn onto the road, cut the lights and wait for their pursuers to pass.

As the SUV approached the turn, he cut the headlights and swung into the access road, tires squealing as they tried to gain traction.

"This is the airport," Arden said.

"I told you. We're flying out."

"I told you, I'm not."

She was.

Even if he had to throw her kicking and screaming onto the Cessna. He'd committed to getting Arden back to her family. He was going to do it. No matter who was after her. No matter what kind of trouble she'd gotten herself into.

No matter how determined she was to keep him from doing it.

He didn't back down from challenges. That was one of the reasons Jace had asked him to do the job. It went deeper than that, of course. They'd served together, fought together. They'd saved each other's hides more than once. Their bond was a brotherhood, and it couldn't be broken. They'd do anything for each other.

Even fly a Cessna through a storm with a passenger who obviously didn't want to be there.

THREE

Intellectually, Arden knew that the one-in-ten-million chance of being killed in a plane crash was much lower than the one-in-one chance of being killed if GeoArray got its hands on her. Once GeoArray got what it wanted, her pursuers would have no use for Arden and no reason to let her live. She'd been on the run for almost two weeks and was certain that with a few more days, she could crack the encryption that protected the files. If she was caught and the files confiscated before she had the chance to extract the information she needed, she'd have no way of proving Marcus Emory was a murderer—and maybe worse. She'd also have no way to prove her innocence.

Yep. Her chances were better on the Cessna, but she wasn't boarding it. She didn't fly. Not ever. She'd find another way out of the mess she'd gotten herself into. Of course, to do that, she had to lose Kane.

She shot a quick look in his direction. He was focused on the icy access road, concentrating on getting them to the death trap of an airplane before their pursuers. If he'd been driving a little more slowly, she would have chanced opening the door and jumping. She probably had a good shot of landing without injury—but not when they were traveling nearly blind in excess of fifty miles an hour, and not with Sebastian strapped to her chest.

She'd have to make a break for it after they reached the plane. Even if she weren't terrified of flying, there was no way she could let Kane bring her home.

As much as Grayson wanted to help her, until she could prove her innocence, she couldn't ask him to take her side against the FBI. Law enforcement was his calling and she would not be the one who caused him to lose his job with the FBI. She wasn't sure what story Marcus Emory had fed the FBI, but his clever move had made her an enemy of the state. She was wanted by the United States government and, by now, possibly a half-dozen other entities.

She had to finish what she'd come to Maine to do.

She had to decrypt the files she'd intercepted from GeoArray. The fact that GeoArray was willing to engage the FBI in its search for her meant that Emory was desperate. Any doubt she'd harbored about the importance of those files was gone. Her gut told her the content of the files would expose the criminal activities behind GeoArray.

She glanced out the back window and saw a vehicle pass the airport access road.

"You can slow down," she said. "They've passed us."

"Not if we want to get to the plane before they realize we've turned off."

"What's the plan once we reach it? We can't just climb aboard and leave."

"Sure we can. It's unlikely other planes are flying out of here tonight. I can be cleared for takeoff in minutes."

"If there's anyone at the tower." And she hoped there wasn't.

"There is. I put in a flight plan for this evening and was given a three-hour window to fly out. We're within that time frame."

"I don't like it," she muttered. "How about you come up with a different plan? Because I already told you, I'm not flying out of here."

He didn't respond.

"Did you hear me?"

"I heard."

"And?"

"I don't change plans. Not when they're good ones."

"Often, it's opinion that determines whether or not something is good," she pointed out. "Your opinion and mine are very different on this issue."

"Are you aiming for an argument, Arden? Because now isn't the time for it."

"There's no time like the present for me to state irrevocably that I think your plan stinks." She didn't care about the argument. She didn't care about his plan. She needed him to think she did. That would put him off guard when they reached whatever death trap, winged vehicle he thought they were flying out in.

He didn't take the bait.

"Who's after us?" he asked instead.

"You asked me that before. I chose not to answer."

"I asked who you were running from. Now I want to know who's behind us."

"Sorry, I—"

"If I'm going to go head-to-head with an enemy, I want to know who the enemy is."

"Ever heard of GeoArray?" she asked. She'd let him think she was cooperating. If he believed she was going along with his plan, he'd be a lot less likely to anticipate her escape.

"GeoArray is after you?" he answered. Obviously he'd heard of the defense contractor.

"Yes."

"Why?"

"I was…helping a friend and I stumbled on some information that GeoArray would rather I not have."

"What kind of information are we talking about?"

"The kind that could get you killed if you knew about it."

"There isn't a whole lot going on tonight that couldn't get me killed," he responded, glancing in the rearview mirror and frowning.

She looked over her shoulder. "Do you see them?"

"No, but once they realize they've lost us it won't take long for them to figure out that we turned into the airport access road." He parked the SUV near a hangar, grabbing her arm before she could jump out.

She could have pulled away. He wasn't holding on that tightly, and she knew how to break someone's grip, but the look in his eyes held her in place.

"Don't try it," he said quietly.

"What?"

"Whatever you've been planning. We don't have time to fight each other."

"We aren't fighting. I'm—"

"You're going to get us both killed, Arden. Is that what you want? Because, if you run, I'm going after you. That will slow us down and give whoever's following us plenty of time to catch up." He released her arm, reached over the back seat and grabbed an army duffel bag, then opened his door.

She opened hers as well, stepping out of the vehicle and shivering as a few flakes of snow landed on her cheeks. She didn't fly, and she especially didn't fly when the weather was bad.

Her plan had been to run as soon as her feet hit the ground, but she couldn't ignore Kane's warning and feel good about it. She glanced at the road running parallel to the airfield, spotting a vehicle creeping along it. It had to be them. It wouldn't take them long to figure out she and Kane were at the airport.

But…

She didn't fly.

She'd have to run, and she'd have to hope that Kane was intelligent enough to stick with his escape plan.

"Don't worry," Kane said quietly. "I've got your pack."

She swung toward him.

She'd forgotten that she'd slipped out of the pack. That wasn't like her. Hesitating wasn't her style, either. She always had a plan. She always followed through on it, and she almost never forgot anything.

Especially not something as important as that pack.

"I'll take it," she said, rushing around the front of the Tahoe to where he was waiting and grabbing one of the straps.

"We're wasting time. I've got it. You want what's in it, you'll have to come with me." He walked away, his strides long and purposeful.

Arden needed that backpack. More precisely, she needed what was inside it. Her laptop. She had, of course, hidden away a second copy of the files for safekeeping, but that laptop contained days of work. In fact, she knew she was close to breaking the encryption wrapped around the files. She couldn't afford to lose all that work. Starting over was not a scenario she wanted to entertain.

"Let's be reasonable about this, Kane," she said.

"If by reasonable you mean we work together to solve your problem, I'm all for it," he responded, stepping into the hangar, his duffel slung over his shoulder, her pack still in his hand.

She had no choice but to follow him right into the belly of the beast.

At least, that's what it felt like when she saw the little tin coffins disguised as airplanes lined up and ready for takeoff.

She felt sick, the thought of getting on a plane and flying into the snowy night making her light-headed.

"You're better than this," she muttered, annoyed with her own weakness.

"What's that?" Kane glanced over his shoulder as he reached the front of the line of planes.

"Nothing."

"You're sure?"

"As sure as I am that I am about to die," she responded.

He either didn't hear or he ignored her.

"We're in front of the queue. That's the good news."

"What's the bad news?" she asked, eyeing her pack and wondering how tightly he was gripping it.

"We're running out of time. Come on. Let's get on board."

The large aluminum hangar door was already open, the Cessna Skyhawk ready to go, having been kept inside the bay to keep ice and snow from accumulating before takeoff. No sign of the dispatcher, but Kane wasn't going to let that slow him down.

He stepped back and took Arden's arm, ignoring the tension in her muscles and the paleness of her face.

"You ready to take off?" someone called.

He turned, watching as the dispatcher walked toward him, a sub sandwich in one hand, clipboard in the other.

"No," Arden responded.

"Yes," Kane corrected.

"Good. Good. You leave now and you'll beat the storm. Otherwise, you'll probably be stuck here for the night."

"That won't work for us," Kane said, with a sense of urgency. "My friend's ex is hot on our heels. I need to get her out of here quickly."

The man nodded his head. "Understood, no problem. Go ahead and load up. I'll contact the tower and tell them you're waiting to be cleared for takeoff." He rushed to his desk, taking a bite of sandwich along the way. Once he'd settled into his chair, he turned to his computer and began typing.

Kane pulled Arden the remaining short distance across the hangar's concrete floor to his plane. There was no sign of the sedan through the open bay doors, but he was certain it would be only a matter of minutes before it would reach the airfield. They needed to be on the plane and on their way before then. "Let's go," he said, sidestepping one of the main wheels and tossing her pack and his duffel onto the rear bench seat of the plane.

Arden stopped short, planting her feet. "Go on without me. I'll find a place to hide."

"That's not going to happen."

"Yeah. It is." She darted away, but he'd anticipated the move and snagged her arm, then, in deference to the cat still hiding under her coat, in one quick motion he hefted her into his arms like a groom carrying a bride over the threshold. He could feel her trembling. This was no joke. She was terrified, and for about two seconds, he thought about finding another way.

Unfortunately, doing that would probably get them both killed. It would more than likely get the guy with the sandwich killed, too.

Kane wasn't in a dying kind of mood, and he sure didn't need any more innocent blood on his hands. He'd had enough of that to last a lifetime. It'd been thirteen years since Evan Kramer had died in his arms and he could still remember the sticky slickness of his second cousin's blood on his hands, the harsh rasp of lungs as he gasped his last breath. A moment in time, a lifetime of regret.

He hoisted Arden up through the open doorway. She was lighter than he expected and, despite her struggling, he still managed to set her down gently on the floor of the plane's cargo area before jumping in after her. Forcing her to do something that obviously terrified her made him feel like the worst kind of jerk, even if his options were less than limited.

"Get out of your coat, and get that carrier off your chest."

Stooping in the threshold of the plane's open door, Kane yelled out, catching the dispatcher's attention once more. "We don't want to bring any trouble down on you, but her ex is dangerous. Be on the alert."

"Got it. I'll lock it down after you leave. And your return flight plan's been approved by air traffic control, so you're good to go. Let's get you out of here before he shows up."

Kane yanked the plane's door shut; the hatch clicked in place as he locked it. When he turned back, Arden was still rooted to the same spot. He quickly unzipped her coat, dropping it on the bench seat with their bags, then helped her remove the carrier from her chest. Cradling the cat in his left arm, he guided her to the front passenger seat, gently pushed her into it and strapped her in with the safety harness. Arden remained quiet as he set the cat's carrier in her lap and wove the lap belt through the blue carrier straps to secure the animal.

Her silence was disconcerting.

She hadn't been at a loss for words since he'd found her at the cottage. The fact that she wasn't talking now was something he'd worry about after he got them in the air.

He stowed Arden's pack and his duffel behind the bench seat, retrieved her jacket and draped it over her lap and chest. She'd closed her eyes and was breathing deeply, mumbling something he couldn't hear.

That was better than silence, but it still wasn't good.

Being ten thousand feet in the air with a woman in full-out panic wasn't much better than being on the ground with a couple of thugs who wanted them dead.

"It's going to be okay," he said, dropping into the pilot seat and starting the engine.

"I told you, I don't fly," she responded, her eyes still tightly shut.

At least she was talking and coherent.

"You do now." He checked the flaps and instrument control panels then pulled the safety harness over his shoulders.

"Oh Christmas tree, oh Christ-mas-tree," she sang, her voice high-pitched and a little off-key.

Maybe she wasn't coherent after all.

"Arden?" He touched her shoulder. Her muscles were taut, her entire body tense.

"Thy leaves are so un-change-ing," she continued. Her voice warbled on the last note, but she kept right on singing. "Oh Christmas—"

"Arden? Are you going to be able to keep it together?"

"I am trying to get to my happy place." Her eyes flew open, and he was looking straight into her sky-blue irises. "*You* are making it very difficult."

"Your happy place is Christmas?"

"It sure isn't this dinky tin can that you plan to fly us out in." She closed her eyes again, continuing her song. "Not only green when sum-mer's here…"

She hit the last note and the cat yowled, joining the song with earsplitting intensity.

At least neither was trying to claw a way out.

He guided the plane out of the hangar, radioing the dispatcher for permission to take off. They began taxiing down the runway. With this load, the plane required about eight hundred feet of runway for takeoff. Maybe a little less if the conditions were perfect.

Tonight, the wind was blowing, a light mix of sleet and snow splattering the windshield.

In the distance, the sedan sped through the airfield gates, then veered toward them, high beams on, picking up speed as it approached. He could only hope they'd beat it down the runway. The plane picked up speed. Six hundred feet. Seven hundred. Kane pulled back on the controls just as the sedan reached the runway. It stopped and the doors flew open.

But Kane was past them, the wheels lifting from asphalt, the plane soaring into the sky. Below, the men were firing. The distinctive metallic pings as several bullets pierced the plane's fuselage left no doubt that some of the rounds had hit their mark.

"Oh Christmas tree, Oh Christmas tree, such pleasure do you bring me!" Arden was nearly screaming the song now, the cat still yowling, the engine roaring.

But they were up, so far away from the gunmen the bullets were ineffective. Whatever damage had been done was done. He assessed the instrument panel, looking for potential trouble.

Arden had stopped her quirky rendition of "O

Christmas Tree." The cat had stopped yowling. The only sound was the whir of the engine. It sounded smooth. No coughs or hiccups, but the fuel pressure gauge dipped and a red light flashed ominously on the panel.

"That," Arden said, jabbing her finger toward the light, "does *not* look good."

"We'll be fine." He hoped. There was a problem with the left flap on the wing of the plane. For now he could still fly, but depending on the issue, his ability to control altitude and speed of the aircraft could definitely be affected—the higher they flew, the worse it would be. More of a concern was the fuel pressure gauge that was definitely reading lower than it should. If they lost fuel pressure, they'd have no choice but to make an emergency landing.

"Define fine," she demanded, her face so pale even her lips were white. She had the bluest eyes he'd ever seen, and a face that was more intriguing than beautiful. She also had a brain that rivaled anyone Kane had ever met—she'd definitely give his academically focused parents and those in their social circle a run for their money.

Lying to her wasn't going to work.

Even if it would have, he wasn't going to do it. Truth was always the best way. Even if the truth was sometimes difficult to swallow.

"A bullet may have hit the wing flap," he said, bracing himself for Arden's full-out panic.

To his surprise, she simply nodded.

"That's what I thought. I suppose you have a plan?"

"Yeah. Get the plane back down and fix the problem."

"Is there another airport close by?"

"It doesn't matter. I won't run the risk of landing anywhere in Maine if I can help it." GeoArray seemed to have connections and resources. He was pretty sure the company could quickly mobilize the troops wherever he put down.

"What if you can't make it out of Maine?"

"We'll cross that bridge when we come to it." And if Kane was reading the gauges correctly, they'd be fortunate to make it across the border into New Hampshire.

FOUR

The plane was definitely listing to the right.

Arden decided not to mention that to Kane. She was certain he'd already figured it out.

"How much time do you think we have?" she asked.

Kane didn't answer, but it didn't take a genius to realize that their time was limited. The red flashing light, the heavily listing fuselage, the slight side-to-side motion—she'd never flown before but she was pretty certain none of that was supposed to be happening.

She took a calming breath. *Mind over matter*, she told herself, and glanced out the window, immediately wishing she hadn't.

The plane continued its ascent over the trees that surrounded the airfield. The lights of the runway were small specks on the ground below them. The town a distant pattern of lights and darkness. It would have been beautiful if she hadn't been terrified.

She had never liked heights and always had an unexplainable and insurmountable fear of flying.

Yet here she was, in the cockpit of a small plane, sitting next to a man she'd met a handful of times, probably already more than a thousand feet above the ground. Flying. Something she'd told herself she'd never do.

Desperate times really do call for desperate measures, she supposed.

On her lap, Sebastian stirred. Arden folded down the jacket Kane had draped over them for warmth, unfastened the carrier's safety flap and peeked down at the cat. Typical of her furry friend, he popped his head up, took in his surroundings and ducked back into the carrier, snuggling into the warmth of her lap.

She'd adopted him when he was almost two. He'd been a nervous cat then, but she recognized the deep-seated curiosity that was kept at bay by his timid personality. She'd known at once he would be hers. The ladies at the shelter had tried to dissuade her, pointed out several friendlier and more confident kittens. But she instinctively knew that no one would be as accepting of Sebastian as she would be. Her own idiosyncrasies had made her more tolerant of differences in others. He deserved a good home with someone to love him despite his quirks. Everyone did.

For the past six years, she had been his family. They'd done everything together.

Now, it seemed like they might die together.

She shouldn't be scared. She knew where she'd

spend eternity. The problem was, she had a lot more living she wanted to do before then.

And then there was the little matter of GeoArray, the fact that without her intervention the company would continue whatever underhanded deals it was making with no one the wiser.

Not only that, but there'd be no justice for Juniper's husband, Dale, and his death would always be considered a suicide, leaving Juniper unable to claim his life insurance policy. Without Dale's income, Juniper would need that money to make a comfortable life for her and their unborn child.

She reached in and petted Sebastian's head, humming a few bars of "O Christmas Tree." It wasn't her favorite song, but it reminded her of childhood, of family nights spent watching Christmas specials with her parents and brothers. Of comfort and love and acceptance.

Christmas was coming.

Would she be spending it with her family?

Or would they be spending it at her grave?

"Death isn't the worst thing a person can face," she said, more to herself than to Kane. "But I'd prefer to not experience it tonight."

He must have heard, despite the loud drone of the engine. "You're not going to die."

"What evidence do you have to support that theory?" Feeling a chill, she pulled the jacket up over her chest and shoulders again, then glanced over at Kane, who was adjusting a headset on his ears with his right hand, his left never leaving the yoke. He grabbed a second set of headphones, passed them to her.

"Put these on. We'll be able to talk without having to yell over the sound of the engine."

A diversionary tactic.

Obviously, he had no evidence, but he didn't want to admit it.

She put the headset on anyway, adjusting the mouthpiece.

The sound of the engine was muffled, and she could suddenly hear the frantic thudding of her heart. Listening to it throbbing in her ears only made her fear more real.

"Can you hear me?" she asked. She was sure he could, but she needed the distraction.

"Loud and clear."

"Can air traffic control hear me, too?"

"Nope, your headset is isolated to this plane. Mine is the only headset that has direct communication with the tower." Kane tapped the instrument panel with his finger, then adjusted some gauges.

"How bad is it?" she asked.

"It's under control, for now." His vague answer was less than satisfactory.

"Can you explain what under control means?"

"Do you always ask for explanations?"

"No. Sometimes I ask for evidence or stats. This time, I want an explanation."

"The plane is maintaining altitude," he said, apparently not alarmed by the fact that they were listing to one side.

"At an angle that doesn't seem conducive to flying," she pointed out.

He met her eyes. "We *are* flying, Arden."

"Stating obvious points isn't helping your cause."

"I think I preferred your rendition of 'O Christmas Tree' to your questions," he muttered, adjusting another gauge.

"I prefer fact to speculation. If we're going down—"

"Every plane goes down eventually."

"That is *not* comforting." She hugged the cat-filled pet carrier to her protectively.

"I'm planning a controlled landing," he responded.

"Planning?"

"I'm also afraid a bullet may have hit a fuel line, so our flight may be cut short." He looked over at her then, his eyes dark, expression guarded.

The dim lights of the instrument panel cast red, orange and green shadows across his face and his dark brown hair. He'd had a military buzz cut the last time she'd seen him; his hair was longer now, falling across his forehead and curling at the nape of his neck in that messy casual way models strove to achieve. On Kane, it looked natural and he didn't seem to be the kind of guy who'd spend time preening in front of a mirror.

"Is that why the light is flashing?"

"That's a warning that the plane's left aileron is malfunctioning. In other words, the flaps on the plane's wing aren't controlling the plane's roll like they should."

"So, the plane can't turn properly?" she guessed, putting the information he'd provided together with other things she'd read over the years. Things about how planes functioned.

And how they failed.

Having a near photographic memory was both a blessing and a burden.

"It can turn. I just have to compensate and allow a much wider turn radius—and a much bumpier ride."

"Human error is the number one cause of small plane crashes," she said, spouting off another bit of information that she'd read years ago. "Most commonly, they run out of fuel because pilots miscalculate distance or fuel efficiency."

"I don't plan to make an error."

"No one ever does," she responded, the fatalistic words ringing in her ears. "JFK Jr. died because of pilot error. John Denver ran out of fuel because he couldn't access a very important fuel selector valve." She'd be better off singing, but she couldn't stop remembering every story she'd ever read about small plane crashes and spouting off the horrible endings like some kind of macabre recording.

"I've got some good news for you, Arden," he said.

"We're landing?"

"This plane has two fuel pumps, and I've already switched to the auxiliary, so you don't have to worry that I don't know how to do it."

"I wasn't worried about that. I was just providing examples and evidence to support my position."

"Which is that we're doomed?"

"I didn't say that."

"Arden, how about you go back to singing?" He adjusted a gauge and frowned. "It looks like we're still losing fuel. I was hoping the bullet hit a tank, but it looks like it hit a main line."

That did *not* sound good.

As a matter of fact, it sounded really, really bad.

She glanced out the window, saw cars and houses far below. "Where's the nearest airport?"

"Behind us."

"But we can't turn around."

"Right."

"So we're going to—?"

"Keep flying and pray we find a spot to land." Kane finished her sentence.

She wished he hadn't.

She would have preferred to create a fictionalized version of what they were going to do. Like—

somehow turn and land on the airfield they'd just left. Or—strap on parachutes and jump from the doomed vehicle.

Although, she wasn't sure she had the guts for that.

Still, anything would be better than sitting in a plane not much bigger than a Barbie Dream Jet waiting for it to go down.

She glanced out the window again; she couldn't help herself.

They were high above the tree line now, tiny lights twinkling through the darkness. House lights. Streetlights. Cars. Hundreds of people going about their business while she and Sebastian and Kane went about the business of dying.

Not that she wanted to be melodramatic about the situation. She was a facts gal. Numbers and figures and stats.

And right now, all those things pointed in one direction.

"I don't suppose you have parachutes on this plane?" she asked casually. At least, she tried to sound casual. She didn't want Kane to know that she was on the edge of full-out panic mode.

"No, but we're not going to need them."

Give me some evidence to support your supposition, she wanted to say, but she kept her lips pressed firmly together, afraid she wouldn't like the answer.

* * *

Arden was taking the news better than he'd expected.

He could let that worry him or he could concentrate on getting them both out of this situation alive.

Kane checked the gauges and eyed the instrument panel. The plane was off its intended course and flying much lower than his flight plan specified. There was nothing he could do about it except search for a place to land.

There were a few lights in the darkness below. Maybe houses or streetlights, but nothing that gave any indication of a clearing big enough to land the Cessna.

Flakes of snow pelted the windshield, cutting down on visibility. He glanced at the GPS to keep his bearings. His original flight plan routed his plane around congested airspace used by commercial flights over coastal Maine, New Hampshire and Massachusetts, then parallel to the Appalachian mountain range, turning back toward the coast as the plane approached Maryland. But Maryland was hundreds of miles away and Lubec was behind them. The malfunctioning aileron made it nearly impossible to change course.

It would be nearly impossible to land, too, but they'd have to do that before they reached the mountain range that was directly in their path. The tallest range in Maine was just over five thousand feet high. Once they hit New Hampshire, the White Mountains would be a threat. At over six thousand feet, those peaks would require him to ascend even higher. Taking the plane's current condition into account, he didn't think that would be safe.

"Is that a mountain range in our path?" Arden was looking at the navigation screen displayed on the instrument panel.

"Yes."

"How close are we?"

"About twenty minutes out."

"Maybe you should call the air tower and find out where we can land before then, because from where I'm sitting, it looks like our chances of getting over the mountains are slim to none."

"I'd rather not contact air traffic control at this point." Or at all, if he could avoid it. Whether Arden liked it or not, his plan was to get them on the ground undetected if possible, call his business partner, Silas, for a ride back to Maryland and deliver Arden DeMarco to her brother.

"Um, okay…why not?"

"Given who's after you, it's safe to assume someone may be monitoring the dispatch system. I don't want to give away our location."

"It's going to be given away when we crash into the side of that mountain," she muttered.

"We'll find a place to land," he assured her. "And we'll probably be better off than we'd be if we'd stuck to my original flight plan and headed back to Maryland."

"You think they'll have people waiting there?"

"They had people in Lubec."

"Right." Shc hummcd a few bars of "O Christmas Tree" and then fell silent.

She'd have probably been happy if he let the conversation die. But to keep her safe, he needed answers.

"Arden, you need to come clean. According to Grayson you're wanted for suspected espionage."

She remained quiet.

"You said you were helping a friend," he prompted.

"Yes."

He waited for more, but she just sat staring at the instrument panel, her coat pulled up to her chin.

She looked young.

She *was* young. Even if there was only a five-year age difference between them, he'd seen things in combat that made him feel a lot older than his thirty years.

She didn't look scared, though. She looked determined and resigned. Maybe a little annoyed that her plans had been derailed. Jace had told Kane to expect that; that she liked to do things a certain way and didn't much care for change.

"What friend?" he prodded, and she met his eyes.

"Look, Kane, it might seem like we're in this together—"

"We *are* in this together."

"Right now, we are. But once we've landed, we don't have to be. You can go back to whatever you were doing before my brother talked you into coming after me."

"No. I can't."

"Sure you can. It's easy. You just rent a car or call for a ride and go back home. I'll go back to what I was doing, and we'll both be fine."

"*You* were hiding from the FBI," he pointed out. "And from a company that seems to want you dead."

"They don't want me dead. Yet."

"What do they want?"

"Encrypted files that I took from them."

"What kind of files?"

"That's a good question. I won't know until I decrypt what I have. That takes time. A lot of it. Which is why I went off the grid. I needed solitude to work."

"And safety."

"That, too. And I was doing fine on both counts. I still would be, if it weren't for Sebastian." She pulled the jacket down and eyed the cat. "And Christmas," she muttered.

"Christmas?"

"Only the best time of the year," she responded, covering the cat again and leaning forward in her seat to peer out the windshield. The snowfall was heavier now, the flakes sliding off the windshield almost as quickly as they landed. "Although, tonight, I'd be happy if it were the middle of summer. The weather is getting worse."

"Yeah. That happens this time of year. Your family has big Christmas celebrations every year, don't they?" Kane began carefully, knowing that he was about to do something he'd probably regret later. He wasn't big on manipulating people. He didn't like using information to get what he wanted, but he wanted to make very sure he and Arden were playing for the same team before he landed the plane and helped her get back to her family.

He'd agreed to find her because of his friendship with Jace. He'd assumed that she had as much integrity as her brother, but she'd admitted she'd essentially stolen encrypted files. Files that he could only presume were classified. GeoArray was one of the largest defense contractors in the country. Much of what the company did was top secret and well guarded.

Arden was on the FBI's most wanted list because of those files. She didn't want to tell him how she'd gotten them or why she took them. If he had to manipulate her to get the answers, so be it.

"What does my family's Christmas celebration have to do with anything?"

"I heard Jace might be home this year."

Her expression didn't change, but he knew the news had gotten to her. He could read it in her quick intake of breath and the sudden tension in her muscles. She knew her brother wasn't scheduled to return from his tour for several months, and she had to know that his early return meant something was wrong.

"What happened?"

"He was injured in an attack a little over a week ago. Their helicopter went down just outside of Syria. Three of his men were killed. He'll be getting an early discharge."

"How bad is he?" she asked.

"He didn't give me many details, and he wasn't sure when he'd be on the medical flight back. He was more concerned about you than he was about his injuries," Kane responded, purposely keeping the extent of Jace's injuries from Arden. His friend hadn't wanted his family to worry.

"He wasn't supposed to be in contact with the family for the next few months. How'd he find out I was gone?"

"Tell you what." Kane adjusted something on the instrument panel and frowned. "How about you ask your brothers?"

"My brothers aren't here. You are."

"I don't know, Arden. Jace called me from a hospital in Munich. He asked me to get in touch with Grayson, said he'd been injured and would be coming home and that he needed me to find you. That was the extent of our conversation."

"I wish I'd known," she muttered.

"You weren't around."

"Are you trying to make me feel guilty?" Her voice trembled, and he thought tears pooled in her eyes, but she didn't let them fall.

"I'm trying to make you see that you're not the only one who is being impacted by the decisions you've made. Jace is returning home. He's planning to be surrounded by his family. He needs to be. He needs time and rest to heal. Not added stress. Plus, if you're picked up by the FBI and tossed into federal prison, you're not the only one who's going down. I am, and maybe Grayson, too."

"That's why I've stayed away. I'm sure they're already watching him. Grayson's like a dog with a bone. I don't want him getting hurt or jeopardizing his job because of me."

"Then give me something to go on. Some information that will help me get you off that list and get Grayson out from under the veil of suspicion."

She hesitated, but he knew he had her. The thought of her brothers suffering because of her actions wasn't something she could live with. All the DeMarcos were like that—all about family, about being part of a team built through shared experience and a lifetime of affection.

As an only child, Kane had never experienced that firsthand. And with parents who preferred their careers to raising a child, he spent more time in boarding schools and later reform schools than he had with his own parents. Aside from summers and school breaks with his grandparents, family bonds and holiday traditions were things he knew little about. He'd been pulled into them through his connection to Jace, but he'd never fully understood them.

"My best friend's husband, Dale Westin, killed himself last month while on a business trip to Boston. He was a network administrator."

"For GeoArray Corporation?"

"Yes."

"What does that have to do with the encrypted files?"

"My friend didn't think he killed himself."

"This is the friend you were helping?"

"Yes. Juniper. She said there was no way Dale killed himself. I knew Dale. I agreed with her."

"Depression can be masked," he said gently. "Some people are very good at putting on happy faces for the people they love." Kane had seen firsthand the devastation that suicide brought down on survivors. It was hard being left behind, wondering if there was something you could have done to prevent it. For years after Evan's death, Kane blamed himself for missing the signs. And they'd been there. Evan had been in a downward spiral since the night his sister drowned, but he'd masked it until the end.

"I know the facts and the figures, Kane. I did the research. But Dale had none of the markers. Not even one, and the way he died, the reason he supposedly committed suicide? It just didn't make sense."

"To people who aren't depressed, suicide rarely does."

"That's not what I mean. According to Geo-Array, Dale had been having an affair with his married boss and she'd coerced him into building a backdoor on the network so she could transfer files outside of the network without detection. Files that she was selling to the highest bidder."

"And they were caught, so Dale killed himself?"

"Supposedly."

"What'd his boss say?"

"She died in a car accident the night before Dale's body was found."

"That's convenient." Kane didn't put much stock in coincidences. Someone was hiding something.

"Yes. All the loose ends were tied up—nice and tidy. By the time I got my hands on Dale's laptop, it was clean. Too clean. Someone had deleted his work-related email and files from his hard drive."

"If the files were already deleted, what was left to find?"

"Getting rid of computer forensic evidence is not as simple as hitting delete and emptying the trash bin. I won't get into the technical aspects of it because I've been told it bores most people. But I was able to find evidence that Dale had discovered the backdoor on the company's networks and immediately reported it to his boss. The email chain I found eventually made it all the way up to GeoArray's CEO, Marcus Emory. Emory asked Dale and his boss to meet him in Boston. They both died on that trip."

"Why not just report what you found on his computer and let the authorities take it from there?"

"I didn't think the email evidence was strong enough to bring to the authorities, so I accessed GeoArray's network, located the backdoor and intercepted some files that were being exfiltrated along with some encryption software I found."

"Exfiltrated?" Kane asked. "Like a military op?"

"Exactly. Just like that." She smiled. "Only instead of sneaking a person out of a hostile environment, I was attempting to sneak the files out of the backdoor without being discovered."

"So you basically hacked into GeoArray's secure network and stole proprietary files."

"Yes."

"And that's why the FBI's after you."

"That's a likely possibility," she agreed.

"What's in the files?"

"I don't know yet. I'm working on decrypting them."

"You didn't think to go to the FBI with what you found—let them decrypt the files?"

"I thought about it, but first, there's no one more qualified than I am to decrypt the files. Second, it's obvious Marcus Emory has the ear of someone in the FBI. I have no idea if that person's an unwitting pawn or a paid accomplice. Going to the wrong person could have meant even more trouble."

"I'm not sure how you could be in any more trouble than you already are," he responded, eyeing the fuel gauge and then the darkness below.

"If I'd trusted the wrong person, I could have ended up in jail with no access to the files, no way to prove my innocence. It could have also implicated Juniper—after all, she suspected GeoArray was behind Dale's death and gave me access to his computer. Sooner or later, they'll put two and two together and see her as a threat, as well."

"If everything you've said is true—"

"Of course it's true."

"—then it stands to reason that, witting or not,

the FBI could pull strings to get the dispatcher in Lubec to track the plane's geo-location beacon."

"So they can get men on the ground before we arrive?"

"That would be my guess."

"If GeoArray catches us, we're both dead. You first, and me after they get their files back. I know you know that, Kane, but I feel the need to reiterate the point. We die. The company gets away with two more murders."

No need for reiteration. He knew exactly what they were dealing with now. And it wasn't good.

He kept the thought to himself.

There were other things to think and worry about. Like the rapidly dropping fuel level. If they didn't descend soon, GeoArray would get exactly what it wanted—the files back and Arden dead, with whatever secret she was trying to uncover buried with her.

FIVE

They were going to have to land soon. Either that or run out of fuel.

The word *crash* came to mind, but Arden didn't voice it. She didn't want to speak into the silence. She was afraid of what she might say.

She'd told Kane as much as she could. Probably more than she should. There were other things—things that she suspected and still hadn't been able to prove—that she wouldn't say. Not to him or her brothers or to the FBI. Even if she said them, no one would believe her.

But she knew what she'd seen: an email exchange between Dale and his boss discussing concern for the security of an unnamed research program. Dale had thought an insider was behind the backdoor he'd found—that someone may be trying to steal GeoArray's research for their own gain. His boss had agreed.

Now they were both dead.

Logic told her they'd been right. Arden just needed to prove it.

It didn't take much digging for her to find that

GeoArray had been awarded a groundbreaking United States government contract to develop a self-improving weapons control system. Arden suspected the research for that system might be concealed under the layers of encryption surrounding the files she'd taken. In her experience, people didn't bother placing that level of encryption around their data unless they were protecting something significant.

Someone had been transferring files outside GeoArray's secure network. Someone was behind Dale's death.

But while she believed that someone was Marcus Emory himself, she couldn't prove it. Yet. As CEO of GeoArray, he definitely had the access and resources to orchestrate the crime. But that alone didn't make him guilty. She needed solid evidence before she could come right out and accuse him, and possibly others in the company, of espionage.

She needed to decrypt the files fast. If she was right, the nation's weapons systems could be compromised and the nation left vulnerable to attack. But it was all speculation. She needed the truth. She needed proof.

Yeah. Running had been her best and only choice.

Taking Sebastian with her had been her mistake.

She scratched him between his soft ears and

felt him purring against her chest. If they died, they'd do it together. Cold comfort, and not really any comfort at all.

She needed to finish what she'd started, and then she needed to get home. Jace had to be severely wounded if he was returning from the Middle East. She knew her brother, and there was no other way he'd come home in the middle of a tour. Though he'd never ask for help, she wanted to be there for him.

But the muted roar of the plane engine, the flashing warning lights and Kane's silence were making her wonder if she'd ever see home again. Kane made another adjustment to the panel, and the plane shuddered.

"What was that?"

"We're descending."

"You've found a place to land?"

He didn't respond, and she knew exactly what that meant: he hadn't.

"If you don't have a place to land, why are we descending?" She wanted an answer that would make sense, one that would make her feel better. One that would hopefully make her believe that they weren't about to crash.

"The low fuel light just came on."

"That isn't the answer I was hoping for," she said aloud, then bit her lip to keep from saying more.

Impulse control. It was a thing. Usually she possessed it, but when she got nervous, she tended to forget that.

He glanced her way, his expression grim. "Would a pretty lie make you feel better?"

"Tell me how I can help," she responded, because admitting that she might have preferred a pretty little lie wasn't going to solve their problem.

"Right now, there's not a whole lot you can do."

"There has to be something," she responded, eyeing the control panel and wondering if there was a user manual somewhere inside the cockpit. If so, she might learn some information that could help. She might be terrified, but she wasn't giving up.

There's a solution to every problem. Pray about it, look for it and be willing to accept it when God finally reveals it to you. Her mother had told her that dozens of times when Arden was a kid— gawky and awkward and too tomboyish to ever fit in with most girls her age.

Following her mother's advice had been easy enough to do when she was a tween and teen. It wasn't so easy to do when she was sitting in a plane that was running out of fuel.

"Is there a user manual somewhere?" she asked, desperate for action.

"You think a user manual is going to solve our problems?"

"It might." She glanced out the window. It

seemed like the ground was getting closer, the dark outline of trees visible through the snow.

"How about we stick to my plan instead?"

"I'm willing to consider it. If I knew what your plan was," she managed to say, her heart pounding so hard she thought it might jump out of her chest. They were definitely descending. Just like Kane had said. Only there didn't seem to be any place to land.

"According to the GPS, we're closing in on Berlin, New Hampshire. If memory serves me, there's an abandoned airstrip about ten miles east of town. If we can find it, we'll land there."

"If it's abandoned, it might not be safe to land on."

"It's safer than flying a plane that's running low on fuel. Keep an eye out for lights, okay? We should be approaching the town soon."

It was busywork. The kind teachers had once given to keep Arden from asking questions and being annoying while other students were finishing their assignments.

She needed the distraction, so she stared out the window, trying to see through the snow. All she saw was gray-black night and swirling flakes.

Please, Lord. Help us find a place to land. Please, get us out of this alive. Please, get me back home to my family.

She felt like a child begging for favors. A child who'd spent a little too much time going her own way this past year. How many times had her parents asked her to attend church service with them recently? How many times had Grayson?

She'd always been too busy with her budding computer consulting business or too tired.

At least, those had been the excuses she'd given.

The reality was, she hadn't wanted to go, because she hadn't wanted to see her ex-boyfriend, Randy. She was afraid if she did, she'd be tempted to call him a lying, thieving fraud. She didn't think that would go over well in the middle of Sunday service. Plus, she hadn't told anyone in her family exactly what he'd done. She'd been embarrassed that she'd fallen for his act. Believed he cared for her when all he really wanted was her brainpower.

When she'd told her family she'd broken it off, they'd all been sympathetic and understanding. She knew that they'd also been secretly relieved and happy about the breakup. Her parents had never clicked with Randy. Her brothers hadn't, either.

She'd met him just before she turned twenty. Having taken university courses while in high school, Arden had already earned master's degrees in both math and computer science and had been invited to the university's cutting-edge research program while she worked on her PhD.

Randy was nearly eight years older, intelligent and heading up one of the university's most prestigious projects. He was just beginning to make a name for himself in the field and she'd been so impressed by his credentials she'd pushed aside her parents' concerns. They'd dated for just about three years, the entire time they worked side-by-side on innovative research projects for the university. She'd thought they made a good team.

Even now, the truth was hard to swallow. Randy was arrogant and self-absorbed. He loved making other people feel stupid. If she hadn't been so enamored with the idea of falling in love, she'd have seen that long before they became a couple.

Too late for self-recrimination, and much too late to go back and change things. She'd learned a valuable lesson from Randy—she wasn't the kind of woman men fell deeply in love with. She was the kind of woman they used.

She scowled, leaning closer to the window, determined to find lights and a place to land, because she did not want to die in this tiny excuse for a plane.

"There!" Kane exclaimed, motioning to the left. "See that?"

"What?" She leaned closer to him, trying to achieve the same line of vision. Just ahead and to the east, tiny lights glimmered through the snow. "Is that the town?"

"Yep. It should be Berlin." He maneuvered the plane carefully, trying to adjust its trajectory. He shifted the controls, and the plane shuddered before quickly stabilizing.

"Are we going to make it to the airfield?" she asked, her voice shaky. She hated that. She also hated that she couldn't help. That she was just sitting there like a ninny while Kane tried to save both their lives.

He didn't respond. He reached past her, his arm brushing her cheek as he pushed a button on the instrument panel and zoomed in on the navigation system.

She caught a whiff of leather and outdoors. It made her think of childhood and the camping trips she and her family had taken. It had been too many years since she'd slept under the stars and listened to the night's music—crickets and owls and leaves rustling in warm summer breezes.

She'd lost her way somehow. She'd gotten off-track and forgotten that her work wasn't the most important thing. Randy had been part of the reason for that. Dating Randy had been easy. He never complained about her work; in fact, he'd encouraged it.

And of course that all made sense now.

She'd broken it off with Randy when she suspected he'd taken her code and sold it to the highest bidder. Some of that code had ended up embroiled in a child-trafficking case Grayson had worked on. She couldn't prove Randy was behind it then, but if she survived this plane ride, she was certain Randy's hands would come up dirty this time—his operational signature was all over the application she'd taken from GeoArray.

The plane shuddered again and every thought of Randy fled.

Below, lights sparkled, barely visible through the swirling snow. Then the town was behind them, and the area below was dark again.

The engine sputtered, and Arden's heart seemed to sputter with it.

"Are we out of fuel?" she asked, the panic she'd been holding at bay threatening to spill out. She could hear it in her voice, and she was certain Kane could, too.

"No." *He* sounded calm. He *looked* calm, his movements confident as he eased the yoke to the left.

"Are we about to crash?"

"I prefer to call it controlled impact," he countered, obviously distracted by the sputtering engine and listing plane.

They were dropping in altitude. She didn't know much about flying planes, but she knew how to read gauges and instrument panels. She'd always been fascinated by mechanical things, and she'd studied airplanes like she'd studied everything. She might be afraid to fly, but she wasn't completely ignorant of how it worked.

"We're going to die," she sighed, the statement popping out before she could stop it.

"Everyone dies," he responded.

"That's obvious."

"It's the truth. If it makes you feel any better, I'm not planning on either of us dying tonight."

"There are three of us on board."

"Cats have nine lives. Your kitty will be fine. We do have a problem, though."

"One?"

He glanced her way, what looked like the beginning of a smile tugging at the corners of his mouth. "A few, but the one I'm currently worried about is our altitude. I can't descend any more quickly without risking the engine stalling. At the speed we're going, we'll overshoot the landing field."

"You're right. That is a problem."

"It's good that we're finally agreeing. That will make things easier when we land."

Probably not.

As much as she appreciated what Kane was trying to do, there was no way she could go back home until she had the proof she needed. And he'd made it quite clear that's what he wanted. Of course that would only be an issue if she and Kane made it out of this alive.

She mentally corrected herself. *When* they made it out alive, she was going to find a way to go off the grid again. She'd been close to decrypting those files. A few more days. That's all she needed. If she could have that, she knew she could get justice for Juniper and Dale, prove her innocence and possibly uncover a plot that could put national security at risk. Then she could go back to Maryland, turn the proof and the files over to Grayson, and let him take it from there.

Kane hadn't missed Arden's lack of response. He was pretty sure she was still planning to run as soon as she got the opportunity. He could have told her that would be a waste of their time, but he had other things to worry about.

They'd already passed the airfield, and the plane was running dangerously low on fuel. He maneuvered the Cessna carefully, trying to adjust its trajectory slowly without stalling the beleaguered engine.

He peered out the window into the darkness below. The abandoned airfield would have been the perfect place to land. Or as perfect as any place could be for a plane in the Cessna's condition. Now that that wasn't an option, he had to reconfigure his thinking, try to come up with another solution to the problem.

The engine sputtered, and Arden nearly jumped out of her seat. She probably would have if she hadn't been strapped into it.

"Relax," he said, keeping his voice calm and even. One of the things he'd learned in the military was that panicking never did anyone any good. Clear precise thinking; clean precise action. That was the way to get out of a deadly situation.

"Relax? You're a funny guy, Kane. I didn't realize that about you." Her voice wavered, but she was trying to stay calm. He'd give her credit for that. Her hands were fisted around the arms of her seat and she was leaning forward, staring out the window. But she wasn't screaming, she wasn't crying and she wasn't getting in his way. And blessedly, she wasn't singing, either.

"I'm full of surprises," he responded automatically, his focus on the approaching ground, the trembling engine and the listing fuselage. He angled the plane slightly, trying to keep it steady for landing. The plane shook and dipped, protesting even the most subtle of adjustments.

It wasn't a good situation.

He needed to land the plane now before the fuel tank emptied. He scanned the ground, looking for a clearing that would give him the best chance of landing safely.

Arden took a heaving lungful of air.

"You okay?" he asked, not taking his eyes off the approaching ground.

"I forgot to breathe."

"That's never a good thing," he said drily.

Apparently, she didn't catch his sarcasm.

"You're right," she agreed. "You stop breathing and you tense up. It's always best to just relax and ride the punch."

"Right," he responded, only half listening.

He glanced at the GPS, and his pulse jumped.

A narrow blue line curved near the top right edge of the map. He eased the aircraft in that direction, fighting the broken flaps and the weather. The riverbanks in places like this weren't easy to land, but he'd navigated worse. He'd flown many rescue missions in Iraq, Syria and Afghanistan. The circumstances of those landings hadn't always been the best, either.

"It's physics simplified." Arden was still talking, spewing facts like she was on a game show trying to win a prize. "In a collision, an object experiences a force for a specific time period that results in the mass of the object changing velocity. That's the basic theory supporting airbags in cars—they essentially minimize the effect of the force by extending the length of the collision. In boxing, it's called riding the punch. When a boxer knows he can't stop a punch to the head, he'll relax his neck and let his head move backward on impact to minimize the force of the blow."

"Arden?" He'd finally managed to fight the plane onto the correct course.

"Think about it this way." She just kept talking. "If you were to—"

"What I'm thinking about is landing the plane. How about you do the same? With both of us focused and paying attention, we have a better chance of walking away from this."

That seemed to do the trick.

She stopped talking, her silence as loud as her voice had been.

He almost felt guilty for cutting off her nervous chatter. Everyone had his or her own way of dealing with nerves. Apparently, when she wasn't singing, she was spouting facts.

"It's going to be okay," he said, trying to reassure her.

"You can't know that. Statistically—"

"Sometimes you have to forget statistics and just trust that God always works everything out for His good." That was a truth Kane had always struggled with. It had taken years to accept that God cared and that He was there. Even in the hard times. Even in the ugliness. And there'd been plenty of that in Kane's younger years. He'd had two deaths on his conscience before he turned eighteen. He'd been the ringleader that night, egging Evan on. The party had been Kane's idea. If he hadn't pressed the issue, Evan would have been watching his little sister more carefully. Lexi would still be alive. Evan, too. Two families had been shattered by that one lapse in judgment. He wouldn't be responsible for shattering another.

"You're right. I know you are."

"So let's focus, okay? There's a river straight ahead of us. I should be able to land there."

"On a river?"

"Do you have a better idea?" Kane pulled back slightly on the controls, forcing the nose of the plane up as he struggled to level it. The landing lights illuminated treetops that rushed toward them at breakneck speed. The effect was dizzying.

Just then, he spotted an opening in the trees almost directly ahead.

The river.

Wide and dark, it loomed ahead. Their only hope. A slight adjustment had the plane angled perfectly, lining up with the flow of the water. The river was wider than he'd hoped, the banks blanketed with more than a foot of snow—remnants of an earlier storm. If they were fortunate, the snow would help cushion their impact.

Reducing the Cessna's speed further, he peered through the falling snow, past the range of the landing lights into the darkness, and prayed for an ideal spot to attempt a landing.

Finally, he saw it. A lazy curve in the river that would allow him to skid the plane over the water. The drag would hopefully bring them to a stop on the banks just before the tree line.

Arden had gone completely silent. No gasping breaths, off-key singing or spouted facts. He could feel her tension, and he could feel his own, the weight of what he was about to do, the responsibility of it, making his muscles taut.

Stay calm.

Stay focused.

That had been pounded into him when he trained as part of the Night Stalkers helicopter regiment.

Pulling back on the steering column, he angled the Cessna's nose up slightly, dropped the aircraft lower and further reduced the plane's speed. The Cessna bumped along the river as its landing gear skimmed the water, bouncing away, then skimming again.

They were moving too fast, the damaged flap making the fuselage list dangerously. He tried to compensate, but they were already down, water spraying, the engine choking. He thought he heard Arden scream, but the sound was masked by the screech of metal as the hull of the craft scraped against low-hanging branches.

They slammed into the riverbank, the explosion of sound deafening, the jarring impact stealing his breath.

Get up! Gather supplies! Get out!

He could almost hear his commanding officer yelling the orders. With the faint scent of fuel spurring him to action, he unbuckled his straps and was up and moving before the metal carcass of the Cessna settled into silence.

SIX

They were alive.

That was Arden's first thought.

Her second was that they needed to get out.

She fumbled with the straps, but her hands were shaking and Sebastian was yowling and she couldn't free herself.

Were they in the river? On the bank?

The headset had flown off. She could hear water splashing against metal and the creaking groan of the wreckage. Cold air flowed in from somewhere, and she shivered, yanking at the strap again.

"Let me." Kane brushed her hands away, and she was free in seconds. He pulled her to her feet and shoved open the mangled door. Water was already lapping at Arden's hiking shoes, licking at the cuffs of her pants.

Were they floating on the river?

"Is there a life raft?" she asked as Kane leaned out the open door.

"We won't need one. Half the cockpit is onshore. Come on." He grabbed her hand, dragging her up beside him.

He was right. They were beached, the tail of the plane dipping into the flowing river, the nose of it pressed into snow and earth.

The plane shifted, tugged by the force of the water. Eventually, the tail would break away or the shore would release its hold, allowing the plane to drift down the river. They needed to be off the plane before that happened.

Kane motioned to the bank. "You think you can make the jump from here to shore? It's not far. Maybe four feet."

"Sure," she affirmed.

She didn't mention that she'd never been much of an athlete. Self-defense? She'd aced it because it was all about physics and movement, but she'd only ever been picked for a team in school because Juniper had so often been team captain.

They'd always looked out for each other.

Always.

And, if Juniper had been there, she'd have been whispering in Arden's ear, telling her that a woman who could throw a two-hundred-pound man could jump three or four feet.

"Are you certain?" he asked.

"No, but I'd rather try and get wet than float down the river in a leaking fuselage." She slid her arms through the carrier straps, tightening it securely to her chest. Sebastian had calmed and settled into the carrier contentedly, obviously un-aware of the fact that he'd just used up another one of his nine lives.

"If you land in the water, you're going to be hypothermic in minutes. Want me to jerry-rig a ramp?" The plane shifted again, and Arden was certain she could feel the force of the water shoving it backward.

"It's simple physics," she muttered to Kane or to herself or, maybe, to Sebastian. "Force. Velocity. Gravitational pull."

"How about you tell me the science behind it after we're out of here?" he asked, reaching into a small cabinet and pulling out a parka and gloves. He put both on, then tugged her hat more firmly over her ears before grabbing her backpack and his duffel. "Do you have clothes in your pack?"

"Yes." Not much, but she could get dry if she needed to.

"Shoes?" He turned off the plane's lights.

"No, but my feet are already soaked. Missing the shore and landing in water isn't going to make them any wetter."

He frowned, reaching back into the cabinet and pulling out several plastic bags. "Wool socks. Gloves. Hats. We can put the bags over your feet after you change socks."

"What about you?"

"My boots are waterproof. I'll be fine. Ready?" he asked. "I'll jump first. You follow."

"Right. Sure." She leaned a little farther out, the frigid air stinging her cheeks. The river in this area was shallow, the glossy rocks beneath its surface shimmering in the crystal clear water. The pebbly snow-dusted shore wasn't far. Beyond that, dense forest blocked the sky. No lights. No houses. Nothing but trees and snow and silence broken only by the rush of the river.

"Arden," Kane said, touching her chin and forcing her to look straight into his face. "If you're too scared—"

"I'm not scared," she said, more to convince herself than him. "Go ahead. I'll follow," she assured him.

She sounded confident.

She sounded capable.

She felt like the kid she'd been in grade school—terrified of public speaking but forced to give oral book reports in front of a hostile audience.

Kane nodded, tossing his duffel onto the shore. He slipped into her pack, and she thought about warning him to be careful, but he was already leaping out, landing lightly on wet rocks.

Effortless.

For him.

She had an odd feeling it wasn't going to be nearly as easy for her. She balanced on the edge of the doorway, took a deep breath and another.

"There's no way to disable the plane's internal

GPS," Kane said calmly. "Every minute you stand there is a minute that the FBI or GeoArray could be using it to find us."

She jumped, taking off like a fledgling bird prodded out of the nest by its mother. No grace. No finesse. Just tumbling through the air and landing, feet slipping, arms windmilling, body trying to go in fifteen different directions.

She'd have landed on her butt in the water if Kane hadn't snagged her wrists and jerked her forward onto solid ground. He released her as soon as she was steady, turning to grab his duffel.

"Nice job," he said, tossing her a couple of the plastic bags and some dry socks. "Take off those wet socks and dry your feet. Then let's get out of here."

"I'm thinking we're about ten miles from town, right?" she asked, pulling off her wet shoes, changing socks and slipping the plastic bags over her now dry feet. She was back in her shoes in seconds, standing up and eyeing the wilderness that surrounded them. If she could get him to relinquish her pack, maybe she could give him the slip and go to ground. It would be easy to drop off the grid out here.

"That's a good estimate," he affirmed.

"Given that the average person walks three or four miles per hour on flat ground, if we factor in the snow and the uneven terrain, our speed will probably be closer to two and a half miles per hour, tops. At that pace, we should hit Berlin in about four hours."

"I won't argue with your math." He smiled, unzipping a pocket in the duffel and pulling out a compass and a couple of flashlights.

"Do you think it's safe to use these?" Arden asked, taking the flashlight Kane offered her. "Assuming the plane's internal GPS is still active like you said, it might not take long for them to pinpoint our location. GeoArray could have helicopters. The FBI definitely does."

"That's a valid concern, but we'll be in the cover of the trees. Besides, we're out in the middle of nowhere and should be able to hear their vehicles coming. Plus, we'll be able to move faster if we can see where we're going."

Arden eyed the dense tree line. "I suppose that's a reasonable assumption. And since there are over seventy species of trees in New Hampshire, with the deciduous varieties less prevalent in the mountains, we should have plenty of cover."

"Now that's a piece of trivia I could never pull from the recesses of my mind." Kane grinned. "I'm impressed."

Although he didn't look like he was poking fun at her, she felt her cheeks redden and was thankful for the cover of darkness. Why couldn't she keep her little factoids to herself?

Kane stepped closer, pulled her hood up over her knit hat and zipped her jacket to her chin.

"Let's move," he said, turning and heading toward the tree line.

She followed, biting her lip to keep more inane facts from spilling out. She was better off spending her time finding a way to get the backpack away from Kane. Once she had it, she could take off. She knew the direction they'd been flying. She knew about how far they were from town. She could make it out on her own, keep Kane from being dragged more deeply into her mess.

First, though, she needed her backpack.

"That duffel looks heavy," she said.

Kane ignored her.

Probably because the duffel didn't actually look heavy, and *he* actually looked like the kind of guy who could have handled it if it was.

"I can carry the pack. That'll make things a little easier for you," she offered.

"No. End of discussion."

"What's that supposed to mean?"

"Jace says you're a genius. I'm pretty certain you know what that means."

"Jace exaggerated." Sort of.

"It doesn't take a genius to understand the word no." He was moving quickly, covering ground at a steady pace.

She kept up, but not as easily as she'd have liked. His legs were longer, his stride covering a lot more ground than hers. She tried to speed up as they reached the tree line, her foot slipping across snow-covered leaves and rocks. She went flying, slamming into Kane's back. She grabbed the pack to steady herself and thought for three seconds about trying to yank it off.

"Not going to happen, Arden," Kane said, and she let her hands fall away.

"If you lose that pack—"

"I won't."

"I'm not sure you understand how important this is."

"I understand perfectly. Now, how about we both quiet down? I'd like to hear anyone who might be approaching."

Fine. She could be quiet and she would be. Eventually, he'd put the pack down, she'd grab it and be on her way. It was a simple plan and an effective one.

If he'd just cooperate with it.

There was no way Kane was going to let Arden wander around in the New Hampshire wilderness alone.

She might think she could find her way back to civilization on her own, but most people who eventually got lost, hurt or killed in hostile environments thought the same. Add GeoArray, the FBI and anyone else who might want to get their hands on her, and Arden's chances of survival became even slimmer.

He'd keep the backpack for now, and probably for the remainder of the time they were together.

Snow was already coating his parka and hat. They needed to move fast, and not just because they were being pursued. Ten miles was a long way to hike in frigid temperature. He'd survived worse, but Arden didn't look like the kind of person who spent a lot of time hiking through snowstorms.

"You doing okay?" he asked.

"Dandy," she muttered.

"How about the cat?"

"Snug as a bug in a rug."

"The terrain is flat through here. Hopefully, it will be the same for the rest of the hike." He pulled his flashlight out, letting the beam dance along the forest floor. The snow was sparser there, the tree canopy holding back some of the swirling flakes.

Behind him, Arden snapped her light on, as well. "The underbrush is thicker than I thought it would be, more deadfall," she commented. "It would definitely be slower going without these flashlights."

"Yeah, we'll make better time with them, that's for sure." His light glanced off a thick wall of brambles, the thorny branches like a barbed wire fence blocking their path.

"That doesn't look good," Arden said, her arm brushing his as she eyed the thicket. "Maybe we should go back to the river and follow it to town."

"We'd be too exposed," he answered. "We'll use the river as a handrail, keeping it in our sight while we stay in the trees. The underbrush is always thickest at the wood line, but once we get a few more feet in, it should be easier going."

She didn't respond, and he pushed into the brush, thorns and twigs snagging his parka as he broke through. She followed close behind, pressing in against his back but not grabbing for the pack again.

She kept up. He'd give her that. No complaints, either.

They moved through the densest part of the undergrowth, sticking close to the tree line. The terrain was flat, the ground sprinkled with snow and dead branches. Berlin would be at the mouth of the river, nestled in the lush New Hampshire landscape. A safe haven or a death trap. Kane wasn't sure which.

If they were fortunate, they'd find an old homestead before they hit the town limits. One that had a barn or an abandoned house on it. Somewhere they could warm up while he fine-tuned the plan. If he had reception, he could call Silas to pick them up, but staying anywhere close to the plane wreckage would be a mistake.

They'd been making steady progress for an hour, ducking under branches, climbing over fallen trees, moving as quickly as they could.

He knew Arden's energy was fading. Her pace

was slowing, and she was falling farther behind. She still didn't complain. She didn't ask him to slow down. She just kept hiking. Once or twice, he thought he heard her singing, but when he looked back, she fell silent again.

"Getting cold?" he finally asked, worried about how quiet she was.

"I passed cold twenty minutes ago," she responded, and he thought her teeth chattered on the last word. He stopped, turning to face her, and grabbed her waist when she nearly stumbled into his chest.

"Sorry," she murmured, her face pale in the darkness.

"Why don't you put on a few more layers? You said you had clothes in the pack, right?"

"We don't have time for that."

"We also don't have time for you to become hypothermic."

"As long as we keep moving, I'll be fine." She tucked a strand of hair beneath her hat and offered a smile that was about as fake as the neon pink Christmas tree his mother used to put up in her sitting room.

"Arden, don't try to be a hero." He slipped out of her pack and would have unzipped it, but a soft sound carried over the rush of the river.

He cut off his light, telling Arden to do the same. He shrugged back into the pack and tugged her close to his side.

"Helicopter," he said, and she nodded, her body stiff, her muscles taut.

The hum of the propellers grew louder. Through the trees, he could see a searchlight arcing over the river. The light swept back and forth across the banks, reaching a few feet into the tree line. The pilot was flying a grid, crossing over the river and then back again. Searching for the plane or for them.

"We need to go!" Arden said, trying to pull away.

He held her still. "We move, and someone on the chopper might spot us. The best thing we can do is stay put until they pass."

"That's counterintuitive," she argued. "If that spotlight hits us, they can land that thing faster than we can run to safety."

"We've got the tree canopy, the snow and the underbrush to hide us. Spotting something on the ground in these conditions is difficult."

"There's such a thing as thermal imaging."

"That's a good point, but with the fresh snow falling, our clothes should be the same temperature as the air, which should make it difficult to spot us." He pulled her down so they were crouching, huddling together in the shadows of a pine tree. The astringent scent of pine filled his nose, the cold air seeping through his coat and pants. He was cold, but Arden must have been colder. He could feel her trembling, hear her teeth chattering.

"That just leaves our faces and of course our breath which will condense and turn to water which is warmer than snow," she said. "We should probably duck our heads down and breathe into our coats."

"Great idea. I wish some of the soldiers I've served with would have thought like you." If they had, he thought wryly, some of them might not have died. He put an arm around her shoulder, dragging her in closer as the helicopter swooped low. They ducked their heads as the spotlight zipped across the forest floor, illuminating dead leaves and white snow. It passed and then returned, seeming to hover yards from where they were.

Arden was still shaking as the searchlight moved across the forest floor, and he wasn't sure if it was from the temperature...or from fear.

SEVEN

Arden wanted to be home. Decorating for Christmas. Calling her mom to ask for cookie recipes. She wanted to be shopping for Christmas presents for her brothers, parents and friends, and for the new nephews that she'd have next month. She wanted to be anywhere but there—shivering with cold, the rotors of the helicopter sending twigs and debris flying.

Kane pressed close to her side, totally in her space, but he was blocking the chopper wind and some of the snow, and she couldn't bring herself to move away.

Finally, the helicopter moved on, zipping above the tree line, its light slashing across the gray-white forest.

"We need to move," Kane said, pulling her to her feet.

"We can't outrun a helicopter," she responded. Sebastian wiggled in the carrier, probably as anxious to be freed as she was to put this nightmare behind her.

"No, but we need a better position. Someplace

that will offer more protection. They may have been getting something on thermal and that's why they were hovering for so long."

"Even covered in snow, we're warm bodies in a very cold landscape," she pointed out. "Of course there *are* an estimated five hundred species of vertebrate animals in New Hampshire, so there are certainly other mammals out here with us. It stands to reason that we could conceal our heat signatures enough to pass as deer. Or moose. There are also bobcats. Foxes. Coyotes." She started listing all the native mammals, the words spilling out like they always did when she was anxious.

"Good point," he agreed, pulling back a heavy pine bough and holding it so that she could walk past. "Hunkering down bought us a little time, but eventually, they'll have troops on the ground as well as the helicopter in the air. It might not be long before they'll send their ground crew to investigate."

He had a point.

She refrained from explaining how good of one it was. She had a bad habit of talking too much about too many things. Or so her ex had said. Then again, Randy had been quick to point out all of her quirks. He'd also been good at telling her the reasons why she needed to change.

In hindsight, she should have kicked him to the curb long before they'd ever become a couple. But she'd wanted what Juniper had had, what her parents cherished. She'd wanted to be part of something more than just herself. She'd wanted to be in love, and she'd convinced herself that she was.

Her fault. Not Randy's.

She was too smart to have fallen for him, but she'd let herself fall anyway. Not that he hadn't helped her along. He'd been so charming when they'd met, so filled with admiration and compliments. He'd bought her flowers and books on string theory.

They'd met at the University Christmas Gala. She'd been uncomfortable in a black cocktail dress and heels that Juniper had insisted she wear. She would have been more comfortable wearing a casual skirt with one of her infamous ugly Christmas sweaters. But Juniper had put her foot down. As a compromise, Arden accessorized with earrings shaped like Christmas bulbs. They did not improve her comfort or confidence level.

When Randy had introduced himself, he'd complimented her on those earrings; she thought that he'd noticed her because of them.

Turned out, he'd noticed her long before that.

She'd been new to the research program but already nipping at the heels of his accomplishments. He'd wanted her in his corner, part of his achievement. He'd wanted her help, her insight, her brain.

He'd wanted her encryption algorithm.

And he'd taken it as his own, using it as a base

to create his own encryption application and key. It was the encryption wrapped around the files she'd appropriated from GeoArray. She was confident whatever was on those files had gotten Dale killed.

And Randy was up to his neck in it. He was dirty and she knew it. She intended to prove it. She just needed a little more time.

She tripped over a thick tree root, and Kane grabbed her elbow, holding her steady.

"You okay?" he asked.

Had Randy ever asked her that?

All she could remember was him asking her about work, about projects, about her ideas and programs.

"Fine."

Except that she felt like a fool. A fool who was now running for her life because of something her ex-boyfriend had done.

The sound of the helicopter had faded; the forest was still again. Fat flakes of snow drifted through the canopy, layering Kane's coat with white. He didn't seem to be hurrying. If anything, they were moving slower than they had been before the helicopter arrived on the scene.

"Shouldn't we speed up?" she asked.

"You said yourself that we can't outrun a helicopter. It's going to swing back around. When it does, I want to be well hidden."

"We're two ninety-eight-point-six-degree pillars moving through a twenty-eight-degree forest. Without a structure to cover us, hiding completely from thermal imaging is a near impossibility."

"Nothing is impossible. I'm looking for anything that can give us enough cover and keep them from pinpointing our location." He pushed through a thicket, holding back thorny branches as she moved through.

A true gentleman. One that held tree branches even when there was no one around to see him or to praise his impeccable manners. Randy had only ever been a gentleman when other people could witness it.

"I really was an idiot," she muttered, stepping over a fallen log, her feet heavy and cold. She was cold all over. Even with Sebastian pressed up against her chest, she could feel the chill of the winter air.

"You are far from an idiot, Arden," Kane said, pulling her to a stop. They stood there for several seconds. She wasn't sure what he was doing, but *she* was listening to the sound of the returning helicopter and to something else. A subtle buzz that seemed familiar. A motor of some sort, maybe.

"What's that?" she whispered.

"A snowmobile, I think." There was no hint of emotion in Kane's voice, no change in his expression. He scanned the area around them.

"It doesn't sound close."

"They'll be here soon enough. The helicopter probably spotted the plane and sent people to check it out." He was moving with a renewed sense of urgency, his hand around her wrist, tugging her through the foliage. They were sprinting now, pushing deeper and deeper into the forest as the distant sound of snowmobiles grew louder.

They were moving fast, but it wasn't going to be enough. Kane knew that, but he wanted to put as much distance between them and the snowmobiles as possible. It was bad enough having the helicopter to contend with. The possibility of being shot by a sniper aiming from somewhere above was a real one, but being apprehended by men on snowmobiles seemed more likely.

If the people tracking them were from GeoArray, they may want to keep Arden alive—at least until they were sure they had their files back. If they were from the FBI, they'd only shoot after they announced themselves.

Arden had gotten herself into some seriously deep trouble. He had to get her out of it. First, though, he had to get them out of this—the forest, the wilderness, the cold.

The sound of the snowmobile was still muted and distant, but the helicopter was heading their way again, the rhythmic thud of propeller blades announcing its return.

Glancing over his shoulder, he saw the searchlight illuminating the trees about two hundred meters behind them. Up ahead, there was nothing but thick tree growth. A large elm had fallen across their path, and he clambered over it, pulling Arden with him.

The root system had left a deep hollow in the ground. Covered by leaves and snow and dead roots, it was a perfect place to hide until the chopper passed.

"Quick, Arden, this way." He jumped into the hole. Reached up to help her down. "Press your back up against the roots of the tree and cover your legs with some snow," he instructed, as he brushed snow over his own legs.

"Cover your face and mouth," she reminded him. She pulled her coat up over her nose and mouth and covered the rest of her face with her gloved hands, leaving just enough space between her fingers to peer out. He did the same.

Within moments, the searchlight from the helicopter was almost on them. "Be still," he cautioned.

He knew from experience that the pilots would be looking for motion, reflective clothing, bright colors—something that was out of place. From their vantage point in the sky, and with the tree cover and snow falling as it was, the pilot's visibility would be limited.

Dressed in dark clothing, with snow covering their legs and boots, Kane and Arden pressed into the shadowy web of roots and waited for the searchlight to reach them.

EIGHT

A wide beam of light swept in a large arc to the left, then right, passing over their hiding place. Kane and Arden remained concealed in the shadows. The strong scent of damp, decaying wood permeated the air.

Arden didn't move, but he could feel her anxiety radiating out. She was scared. She should be. They were mere moments from being discovered.

Hopefully, the roots, snow and old wood would keep their thermal temperature from registering. Hopefully, the chopper would keep going. Hopefully, the snowmobile driver wouldn't happen upon the tracks they left and would have no idea where they were. They'd have even more time to put distance between themselves and trouble.

Hopefully, but Kane wasn't counting on it.

One thing he'd learned during his years in the military: never take safety and security for granted. Anything could happen at any time. He'd learned to be prepared for it.

Somewhere close by, a small herd of deer was startled from hiding. The animals bolted through the darkness just ahead of them, jumping over logs and stumps, weaving through the snow-coated trees and disappearing deeper into the woods. A few passed close enough to jump over the downed tree where Kane and Arden took refuge.

The movement of the deer was caught in the searchlight. The beam of light passed quickly across Kane and Arden's hiding place, shining briefly on one or two of the fleeing deer before it continued its probing search.

The light moved farther away. They were no longer in the direct path of discovery. The rhythmic thump of propeller blades receded.

Kane stood cautiously, motioning for Arden to remain concealed.

The searchlight was barely visible through the trees. The forest around them was once again dark. Kane pulled himself out of the hole, then reached down to help Arden climb out.

"What should we do?" she asked. "They're going to assume we're headed downriver—they'll probably be waiting for us on the outskirts of town."

Kane had been thinking the same thing. Once their tracks were discovered, it would become evident that he and Arden were paralleling the river and heading to town. Even if their tracks weren't found, that course seemed the only logical choice.

And that's because it was the only logical choice. Upriver was away from the closest town. Crossing the river was out of the question. One thing was certain: they couldn't stay where they were. Not only because the woods offered no protection from the elements, but because there was no doubt in his mind that the helicopter had left a trooper or two on the ground. It's what he would do if the situation were reversed. Between the ground troops and the snowmobiles, it would be very difficult to escape detection.

Kane surveyed the area. Up until this point, their chosen path had been relatively flat, minus a few drainages that ran off the mountain into the river. Deeper in the woods, the terrain sloped gradually up as the mountain rose from the valley.

It would not be an easy hike.

It would also not be an obvious choice.

If they headed into the forest and away from the river, the heavy snowfall might cover their tracks before anyone on the ground reached this area. The assumption would be that he and Arden had continued along the easiest route. Doing the unexpected would buy them time and, possibly, allow them to escape.

"You're right. I think we need to change course," he said.

"You're thinking of heading up the mountain, right? Doing what we shouldn't and hoping that throws them off our trail. Buys us some time."

"It's the best plan I can come up with on short notice," he said honestly.

"It's better than my plan," she responded.

"Which is?"

"Click my heels together three times and repeat, 'There's no place like home.'" She smiled, a quick curve of the lips that was echoed by the amusement in her eyes. She might be half frozen and running for her life, but she still had a sense of humor. Not something he was used to seeing in the high-stress environment he'd worked in. Stone-cold seriousness or morbid sarcasm seemed to carry his comrades through. Arden's kind of humor—the soft and easy and light humor—was a refreshing change of pace.

She was refreshing.

She was herself and nothing else.

That's how Jace had described her when he'd asked Kane to track Arden down. Obviously, he hadn't been exaggerating.

"You're an interesting person, Arden," Kane said, heading away from the river and toward the mountain slope.

"So I've been told," she muttered.

"That's a compliment."

He glanced her way, met her eyes, saw her smile again.

"In that case, thanks. Although, I'm surprised you didn't notice when you were at family functions with Jace."

"I was noticing other things."

"Like?"

"How kind your family is to one another. How talkative they are. How deeply connected you all seem to be." But of course he'd noticed her, too. She'd intrigued him from the start, though he wouldn't let himself go there. She'd been Jace's younger sister after all—dressed in crazy Christmas sweaters or bunny-eared hoodies, flitting from one person to another, completely unaware of her allure, her cold-eyed boyfriend hovering nearby.

"You don't have a family?" she asked, her breath puffing out into the snowy night.

"Most people do," he said, wishing he hadn't mentioned her family and that she hadn't asked him about his. His parents were good people. They tried. But he'd never lived up to their academic standards. He'd never been the kind of kid who'd craved knowledge, who'd aced tests, who'd been at the top of his class.

"Hmm, another nonanswer I see," Arden said, panting a little, struggling a little.

He knew he was moving fast, and he knew she could barely keep up, but the buzzing engines of snowmobiles were growing louder. Keeping ahead of the enemy was paramount to survival.

"Tell you what," he responded. "We can discuss my family once we're safe. For now, let's conserve our energy for the hike."

She didn't argue.

He was worried about what that might mean.

He had no idea when she'd eaten last, how much she'd slept the previous night. He knew she'd had self-defense training with her brothers, but he had no clue as to how fit she was.

He could push her as much as he wanted, but her body would only go for as long as it could. Then she'd be down, and he'd have to carry her and her cat out of the wilderness. Not impossible, but it would complicate things a lot.

Getting out of this mess alive was already complicated enough.

Arden followed closely behind Kane, matching his quick pace step for step. She didn't want to slow them down any more than necessary. It was bad enough that Kane was in this predicament because of her. If she got him caught and killed, she'd never forgive herself.

Of course, if she were dead, she wouldn't have to worry about that.

And, she knew if they were caught, she would die. Eventually. Once GeoArray had the files, eliminating her would drastically reduce the company's chances of being exposed.

Cold wind whipped at her cheeks and sliced through the fabric of her pants. She gritted her teeth to keep them from chattering and kept walking. She had no choice.

This wasn't just about Kane's life. It wasn't about hers. If she was right, and the research Dale and his boss referred to in the email was related to the self-improving weapons control system, it was about national security. And that could mean it was about the lives of millions of people.

Even thinking it seemed melodramatic. She couldn't imagine speaking the suspicion out loud. She needed proof, and she needed time to get it.

She wasn't sure they were going to get that.

She could hear the snowmobile moving closer. More than one by the sound of it. She could picture half a dozen armed men and women speeding across the snowy landscape while she and Kane trudged along.

"We need a vehicle," she panted, surprised at how breathless she was.

"True," he responded.

Short. Simple. Abrupt.

"We need a plan to get one."

"Arden." He stopped short, swinging around so that they were face to face. The snow had turned to pellets of sleet, and they pinged off his shoulders and hat. He had a strong face and gorgeous eyes; the kind of looks that most of her friends would have gone crazy over.

The kind of guy that would never give a tomboyish computer nerd like Arden a second glance.

"What?" she asked.

"You need to save your breath. We've got a long hike ahead of us, and you're wasting energy talking."

"If we had a vehicle—"

"We don't. We're in the middle of the New Hampshire forest. The town is miles away."

"There are other places we could get a vehicle. We're in the White Mountains after all—even though much of it's national forest, there's still a lot of acreage owned by private citizens. There could be vacation cabins nearby, active timber operations, campgrounds."

"You're right, but without a map of the area we're running blind. Without divine intervention, we could search this forest for days and never stumble on any signs of civilization. We don't have time to do anything but stay the course. We need to keep moving until we're certain it's safe to angle back toward town. There's no question we'll be able to get our hands on a vehicle then."

"There's always time to pray."

Kane smiled. "Right again. And we don't need to voice our prayers for God to hear them."

She couldn't help but smile back. "Point taken. I'll save my breath."

He started walking again. Jogging really. His pace even more brisk than it had been. The ground and vegetation were slippery with ice. The temperature had dropped significantly since they'd landed. Maybe as low as twenty degrees. Thankfully, with the pace they were keeping, she'd warmed up. She imagined any wildlife that thrived in the brutal New Hampshire winters had hunkered down for the night, curled up against the storm.

Right about now, she wished she were curled up with a nice thick quilt and a cup of vanilla bean tea. Unfortunately, at this exact moment, the best she could do was pray for divine intervention and, barring that, hope they'd be able to slip into town unseen and find a warm place to take shelter until they could rent a vehicle and get away.

Kane pressed forward as Arden sent up her silent prayers. He was right, of course. They needed to conserve their energy.

Well, *she* needed to. She wasn't sure about him. He seemed to be moving along without effort, no gasping breaths or stumbling steps. Definitely fit. But why wouldn't he be? The company he and Jace had started was all about training security forces and offering protection to a variety of clients. That meant being fit, smart and ready for trouble.

She was smart. As for the other two things... She obviously would not get a job on their team.

Which was fine. She had no desire to go into that kind of physical security. She was more interested in computers. The hash analysis she'd run yesterday had been something most people would have no clue about.

She knew Randy took shortcuts in his work and she figured he'd used a public key system as the base for the second layer of the encryption program wrapped around the files. After running the hash analysis, she'd identified some known code that she'd modified and applied to her first attempt at a decryption algorithm. It hadn't worked, but she believed she was almost there—a breakthrough was imminent.

Randy and Arden had collaborated on a number of research projects and she understood his thought process like no one else. She also understood his weaknesses. His codes would be impenetrable for most analysts, but they would not hold up against Arden's scrutiny.

And they both knew it.

It probably pained him to tell GeoArray's CEO, Marcus Emory, that the files were in her hands. But she was certain Randy had told him because it hadn't taken the company long to send someone to ransack her town house. There was no other person that could have recognized her operational signature so quickly.

The snowmobiles were getting closer, the sound louder in the hushed stillness of the snowy forest. The sloping terrain was difficult, her feet constantly slipping on ice-crusted snow. Arden struggled to control her breathing.

Kane reached back, grabbing her and pulling her along. He still wasn't out of breath, and he still didn't seem cold or tired.

He dragged her onto a narrow deer trail that wound its way through thicker foliage. The ground had been trampled down and their footprints would be more difficult to see there. At least, that's why she thought he'd headed that way. They sure weren't going to be less difficult to spot. Not from the air.

The deer trail was definitely easier to follow. Kane took advantage of this by pushing them harder. They were almost running through the woods. As much as anyone could run contouring up an icy, snow-covered side of a mountain.

A sudden flash of light through the leafless trees in the forest below caught her attention. "They're coming," she panted.

He looked over his shoulder. "I see them. They're not going full speed and there's definitely more than one. They haven't spotted our tracks yet. But when they do, they'll be able to follow them easily."

They raced through the woods, following the deer trail as it wove up the mountain. Within minutes, the snowmobiles were directly below them. Kane pulled her behind a tree while the vehicles continued to move steadily forward, the drivers shining handheld lights on the ground and into the trees.

"They're definitely searching for footprints," he said quietly, leaning his head toward hers. The warmth of his breath touched her cheek. She felt comforted by that and by him. Odd, because she usually liked to handle problems alone. She didn't care to have other people messing with her plans, and she sure hadn't ever thought she'd need anyone to save her life.

Right now, though, she needed Kane, and he needed her to keep her head screwed on straight. No panicking. No chattering. No singing. No running straight into more trouble. She had to be smart. She had to think.

"It isn't going to take them long to catch up," was all she managed.

"Don't worry, I've got an idea."

"Good. Great. Want to explain before they arrive?"

"That," he said, pointing into the sky, "is my plan."

"What? Sprout wings and take off? We already tried the flying thing. It didn't work out."

"Not flying. Climbing." He stopped beneath the broad branches of an oak tree.

She skidded to a stop beside him. Lungs heaving, legs trembling, thankful to not be moving.

Until she finally saw where he was pointing.

There was a structure in the tree. Some kind of wooden platform pounded into thick branches about eight feet off the ground.

"That looks rotted. And dangerous."

"There's no time to second guess. It will hold. They're closing in fast, and we need to get off this trail before they follow our tracks right to us."

Icy snow was still falling, layering fresh white

over their very visible footprints. He was right. This was their best chance.

She followed Kane around to the far side of the tree. A few ice-covered two-by-fours had been hammered into the trunk, forming a makeshift ladder of sorts. The person who'd built it was obviously tall. The bottom rung was a good three and a half feet off the ground, with the rung above it just out of her reach.

She didn't have time to ponder how she was going to get on the two-by-four. Kane grabbed her waist and lifted her up, setting her feet on the lowest rung. She felt her boot slip as she steadied herself, grabbing the slippery rung above with her gloved hand. Somehow, she managed to hoist herself up.

She reached the last rung of the ladder and scrambled up onto the platform.

Kane wasn't behind her.

He wasn't climbing.

In fact, he was moving away. She crawled to the edge of the deer stand and looked down. Sebastian let out an unhappy meow. Poor guy was probably hungry. He was always hungry.

She patted his head, searching the area beneath the tree until she found Kane. "What are you doing?" she whispered as loudly as she dared.

"I'm covering our tracks here so they can't tell we left the trail. Then I'll run up the trail a bit before curving off into the trees and circle back,"

Kane replied. "There won't be enough snow to cover our tracks completely, and I don't want them to realize we bailed here."

"What if they catch you?"

"You'll be fine."

"I'm not worried about me. Well, I am, but I'm also worried about you. They don't need you. You'll just be collateral damage."

"They aren't going to catch me." He sounded confident. He looked it, too, silhouetted in the gray winter night, his shoulders broad, his body muscular. He looked like a hero from one of those action movies she'd watched when she was a kid—tough and rugged and ready to walk through a barren wasteland to save the world.

Only this wasn't a movie. If GeoArray's thugs were on those snowmobiles, he'd be killed. "Kane—"

"No singing, Arden." He'd already turned away, was heading back toward the trail. "No humming. No clicking your heels together. Stay quiet until I get back."

That was it.

He was there and then he was gone. She thought she saw his shadowy form moving along the trail, but she wasn't sure if it was him or trees blowing in the gusty wind.

She shivered, pulling Sebastian a little closer, forcing her mind to something other than Kane—

the computer system. The encrypted files. The headway she'd made.

She started spinning programs through her mind, mentally testing variables, imagining their results on the encrypted file. The sound of snowmobiles grew louder. The snow fell in even heavier sheets and covered the trail and the trees and the little hunting stand where she and Sebastian waited.

Kane sprinted up the path, mentally counting his paces and tracking his direction of travel. He didn't want to get lost. He couldn't afford the time it would take to use his compass and get himself back on course. He also couldn't afford to leave Arden for too long. She was smart, funny, quirky. Unpredictable. That last one worried him.

He wanted her to stay where he'd left her.

He wasn't sure if she would.

He also wasn't sure how well she'd be hidden. The tree stand was great as long as the guys on the snowmobiles weren't looking too carefully. If they shone searchlights toward her location in the trees, they might just see some of the tracks he and Arden had left as they ducked off the deer path. It had been impossible to obscure them all.

He ran up the trail about seventy meters before taking a sharp left, leaping from the path into the thicker tree cover and doubling back. Jumping deadfall, breaking through the ice-covered snow, he sprinted all out.

He found the base of the tree where he'd left her. Scrambled up, relieved to find her there. Her black clothes blended with the darkness, but her face was stark against the night, and he could see her eyes widen as he climbed onto the platform.

"You made it," she whispered. A smile curved her lips, softening the angles of her face.

Something about that smile reminded him of all his childhood dreams of having someone to come home to. Someone who'd be happy to see him when he returned. It had never been that way with his parents. He'd always been the third wheel to their partnership, the unexpected surprise that had changed everything.

He'd thought he'd finally found that someone to come home to when he met Ellen.

He'd been stationed in Georgia for flight school. She'd been waiting tables in the officer's club and studying accounting at the community college. Beautiful and outgoing, she'd had an infectious laugh. He'd fallen for her. Hard. They'd maintained a long-distance relationship during his first tour of duty. Gotten engaged while he was on home leave.

But it didn't take long for rumors to surface. When he'd confronted Ellen, she'd admitted she needed someone to be there with her, and for her, every day. Something he just couldn't do. Not then.

He'd joined the military to atone for Evan's death. For Lexi's. When push came to shove, Kane's obligation to Evan's family was stronger than his love for Ellen. His obligation to them was a driving factor in every decision he made.

After breaking off the engagement, Kane had jumped from relationship to relationship, woman to woman, avoiding commitment. Afraid to put his heart into something that just wouldn't last. After a while, he'd gotten tired of that.

He and Jace had met by then, and Jace had set an example of gentlemanly honor, of respect, of work ethic. He'd talked to Kane about things that mattered—faith and hope and believing in a God who was bigger than every failure.

Those things had sunk in deep.

Kane had stopped playing the field, but never met the one woman he could share his life with. He figured he might never settle down with a family of his own. He was fine with that, but sometimes he wanted more than an empty apartment when he returned home at night. He wanted more than silences at dawn when all the memories woke him. Of Evan and Lexi. Of others lost later, in combat.

He wanted something like what he saw in Arden's smile.

He frowned, pressing in close so that they were

shoulder to shoulder. The tree stand was small but sturdy.

"I can see their lights," she whispered.

He shimmied past her along the large branch that hung out over the trail. "They're almost here. Get to the ladder, stay hidden and be ready to move when I do."

She nodded, carefully maneuvered her body around the trunk of the tree and lowered herself onto the topmost two-by-four. She waited, poised to descend at his signal.

The hum of engines grew louder. The light from an approaching vehicle reflected on the adjacent trees just before it rounded the bend. He remained motionless, silently calculating the vehicle's speed as it rounded the curve in the trail. It sped by the tree, the driver unaware of their presence.

Kane watched until it disappeared around another curve in the trail. Moments later, a second vehicle approached the bend. He readied himself. He'd have to time his move perfectly if he wanted to pull this off.

The snowmobile approached, this driver taking the curve more cautiously—clearly not as confident in his driving skills. The slower speed would work to Kane's advantage.

He waited until the guy was right behind them, and then he moved, launching himself out of the tree. The driver must have heard him. He looked up, reached for something beneath his jacket.

Too late.

Kane was already on him, the force of his movement sending both of them skidding across the snowy trail, colliding into a young tree. The other man took the brunt of the impact, his helmet glancing off the tree, his left shoulder taking most of the blow.

With the tether switch ripped from the snowmobile, the engine cut off abruptly. The vehicle's forward momentum carried it a few feet farther up the trail before it skidded to a stop.

Kane pulled himself off the driver, who lay motionless in the ice-crusted snow—his left shoulder lodged against the tree. Crouching over the fallen man, Kane removed his glove and checked for a pulse. It was there, strong and steady. The man's helmet, scraped on its left side, appeared to have deflected the initial hit to the tree.

The high-end black tactical gear the man wore screamed of private security. There was no time to check for identification or to wait to see what they could learn once the man gained consciousness.

Kane guessed he was a GeoArray-hired thug, but he couldn't know. And he didn't dare wait around to find out.

Arden had already climbed on the snowmobile.

Kane reached down and quickly unhooked the kill switch tether cord from the man's belt and tossed it to Arden.

Ahead on the trail, the hum of the first snow-mobile abruptly stopped.

"That's not good," Arden muttered, turning the key in the snowmobile's ignition. The vehicle sprang back to life.

"Let's get out of here." Kane hopped on behind her, sliding an arm under the cat carrier and around her waist.

"Where to?" she asked, turning in a tight U and facing back the way they'd come.

"There was a fork in the trail a while back. Go there. We'll take the right branch and hope we can lose him on it."

"All right," Arden responded. "Hold on."

She gave it full throttle, navigating the snow-mobile back along the deer trail. Totally focused. No singing. No humming. No list of things that could go wrong or right.

He imagined this was the way she did her job—with absolute dedication.

She found the fork without any help from him, the snowmobile skidding to the right. The steep trail would bring them farther up the mountain and turn them back toward town. They'd lost some time backtracking, but they had a vehicle now. They'd ride the snowmobile as far as they could, then go it on foot. If they could stay ahead of their pursuer, they just might make it out of this without any blood being shed.

Kane prayed that would be the case. He was

prepared to do whatever was necessary to keep Arden out of the hands of GeoArray Corporation, but he'd rather avoid a shoot-out. GeoArray wasn't the only entity after Arden. The FBI wanted her. Local authorities might be pulled in to apprehend her. At a distance, it would be impossible to distinguish the law from the lawless.

He'd been a sharpshooter in the military. He was well trained. He could hit his target. But he had enough innocent blood on his hands.

His memories were vivid and unrelenting. Lexi's blue lips, the gray tint of her skin as he pulled her from the bottom of the pool. The strong scent of chlorine. Water dripping from his face as he'd tried to breathe life into her.

Through Evan's tears and pleading to God, through their friend Tyler's panicked phone call, Kane had counted breaths. Counted compressions. He could never forget. Every moment was etched in his mind. She'd been four years old. Even his dreams were not safe from remorse. He'd prefer not to add an officer of the law to his list of regrets.

Arden slowed the snowmobile and gestured farther up the mountain. "See that? Looks like some-one cleared the trees. Do you think it's a road?"

He could see the area. The trees were sparse against the black-gray sky. These mountains had once been filled with logging camps, so it was likely that old logging roads still crisscrossed the landscape. If they were looking at a road, there might be a cabin at the end of it. Maybe an old vehicle with enough gas in it to hot-wire and drive.

"If you think you can get this thing up there, we can check it out."

She nodded, gunning the engine again.

They left the deer trail, bounced along snow-covered leaves and over thick root systems and deadfall, and finally burst out onto a road. Although coated in a layer of snow, it showed signs that vehicles had passed through earlier in the day. Tire tracks were coated with a fresh layer of icy snowfall. He wasn't sure if it was an actual paved road or some sort of access road, but it was definitely a road.

If they went downhill, it would probably bring them to Berlin faster. The thought of making it to town was appealing. Arden was cold. Running on fumes. But in reality, going downhill might bring them closer to danger. For sure, it was the direction anyone following them would think they'd gone.

"Up or down?" Arden asked, her voice tight with tension.

The first snowmobile had gone silent. The driver had either stopped to help his fallen comrade or he'd come up with a different plan of attack. Either way, Kane and Arden needed to keep moving.

"Up," he said.

She gunned the engine again, speeding along the road, passing old wooden signs that pointed the way to camping areas.

As they rounded a bend in the road, the road forked off in two directions. At the intersection, three wooden arrows on a painted post pointed them in different directions. Two of the arrows pointed up the mountain, identifying Milan Hill Picnic Area and the fire tower. The third arrow pointed left and announced the campground office. It was off-season; the office would likely not be staffed.

"Left?" Arden asked, heading in that direction before he answered.

They were finally in sync, working together as a team, thinking in the same direction. He'd experienced the same on the battlefield, the connection between the men and women there almost mystic in its intensity.

The need for survival trumped just about everything else.

Except love. He'd seen how powerful that could be, and he knew how much people were willing to sacrifice for it.

Arden pulled up in front of a small wood-sided cabin. Several outbuildings were scattered nearby. A freestanding display case stood near the cabin—a map of the campground inside it. Nearby, a long carport housed three pickup trucks. Two were new, with shiny paint and gleaming windows. Both were Parks and Recreation vehicles.

The third truck was older, with a dented hood and cracked windshield. There'd once been a New Hampshire Parks and Recreation logo on the door, but someone had sprayed a light coat of green paint over it. The words *For Sale* had been scrawled across the top of the front window, the lettering old and nearly worn off.

If it worked, they could take that. Its age should make it easy to hot-wire. If Kane had to, he could syphon gas from one of the other two vehicles.

He hopped off the snowmobile and tried the truck door. Unlocked. Just like he thought it would be. The interior was as worn as the exterior, but the inside light came on. Hopefully an indication that the battery was in working order.

He tossed his duffel bag behind the seat, then slid into the driver's seat, pulling out his Swiss Army knife.

"What are you doing?" Arden peered into the truck, her face dripping with melting snow, her hat listless and sopping wet. She'd unzipped her jacket and freed Sebastian, holding the giant animal in both arms.

"Big cat," he commented as he opened the ignition switch.

"That's not an answer to my question."

"I'm hot-wiring the truck."

She frowned. "We can't steal a truck, Kane. It's against the law."

"Would you rather stay here and get caught?"

"No." She set the cat down. "Do your business, Sebastian, and be quick about it," she said, then tugged at the pack Kane still wore. He grabbed her wrist. No way was she getting the pack. Not until he had her somewhere safe.

"We don't have time for this," he muttered, looking straight into the bluest eyes he'd ever seen.

"I'm just grabbing some cash." She pulled back, waving a wad of bills at him. "How much do you think this thing is worth?"

"Arden—"

"Seriously, Kane. How much?"

"A couple hundred. At most."

"Okay." She pulled out a few bills and shoved the rest back in the pack. "I'll be back."

"Don't go far," he warned. "I'll have this started in a moment."

"I won't." She was humming as she jogged away, the cat scurrying along beside her. She shoved the money through a mail slot in the cabin's door. He tracked her movements as she walked to the display case.

She must have felt the weight of his stare. She met his eyes again.

She was lovely. The unwelcome thought popped into his mind. He pushed it out just as quickly. Arden's brother was his best friend. There was no room for thoughts like that.

"You're not going to ever get done if you don't get started," she pointed out. "And you really do need to get started. I think I hear the snowmobile again."

He did, too, the distant hum of the engine echoing through the snowy clearing.

It took him seconds to get the truck started, the engine sputtering for a few moments before it sprang to life.

He checked the gas gauge. Over half filled. That was plenty to get them past Berlin. There were other small towns interspersed through the region. They could fill up when they reached one. He shrugged off the pack and tossed it behind the seat with his duffel.

A flash of light caught his attention, and he glanced at the tree line. Definitely a light, there and gone as it was blocked by trees and revealed again.

"Arden!" he shouted, but the passenger door was already opening and she was sliding into the vehicle. Cold air and snow seeped in with her. Sebastian was in his carrier again, eyeing Kane balefully.

"Hurry," Arden huffed, slamming the door shut.

"I plan to," he responded. He pressed on the gas and prayed that the old truck was more reliable than it looked—and that it could outrun a snowmobile and whatever else might be waiting for them when they got off the mountain.

NINE

Arden was scared.

She could admit it.

She'd seen the campground map. She'd memorized it. She knew exactly how far up the mountain they were and exactly how sharp the horseshoe curves were that would lead them down.

In the best of weather with the best of road conditions, they'd have to take those curves slowly. The weather was horrible. The road was icy, and Kane was racing along like they were on an open stretch of highway in the middle of the desert.

Yeah. She was scared, so of course she opened her mouth and started talking.

"Velocity is the change of position relative to time. Based on the speed we're going and the fact that the first horseshoe curve we'll encounter is roughly three miles from the campground, we have a good shot of becoming airborne in the next couple of minutes." The words just kind of spilled out, and she was certain Kane's lips curved. His focus was on the road, though. He didn't even glance in her direction.

"Are you asking me to slow down?"

"Statistically speaking, the chance of you making the first curve at this rate of speed is slim to none." There she went again. She pressed her lips together, sealing in more information that wasn't going to help their situation at all.

Kane was smart. He could have figured it all out without her spiel.

To his credit, he just nodded, easing off the accelerator and slowing down.

"You know, Arden," he said, and she braced herself to get an earful. How many times had Randy pointed out that she'd embarrassed herself and him by saying too much, offering too many details, talking incessantly? Too many.

But he was a jerk, so she really shouldn't care.

Except that she knew he'd been right. She did talk a lot about the things she liked. And she liked a lot of things.

"What?" she finally asked. She told herself she wasn't going to care about Kane's opinion any more than she should have cared about Randy's. But of course she was lying.

"Until tonight, I'd never met anyone who could make me smile while I was running for my life."

"I'm glad I could amuse you," she replied, her cheeks hot with embarrassment. Amusing other people was something she excelled at.

"I didn't say I find you amusing, Arden. I find you pleasantly surprising," he continued. He took the first steep curve without difficulty, the truck only shimmying a little on the ice-and snow-crusted road. "I knew you were smart, but you're so much more. The way you handled the snowmobile back there, the fact that you took the time to leave money for this beat-up truck just because it's the right thing to do. The way you've pushed yourself all night. It's refreshing. You're refreshing."

They'd reached a long stretch of gently curving road, and he did glance her way. Just a quick look, but she saw something in his eyes that made her breath catch. She'd never ever seen it in Randy's. Admiration mixed with respect. That's how she'd describe it if she was asked.

She looked out the window, focusing on the grayish night, the ice-covered trees, the swirling snow. Anything but Kane. There was something different about him. Something down to earth and honest that made her want to talk more, ask questions, find out who he really was when he wasn't hanging at the edge of her family's holiday celebrations.

She wasn't going to do it.

He'd be too easy to fall for. And she wasn't ready for another relationship. Being made a fool of once was more than enough.

"There's another horseshoe curve coming up," she said, eyeing the dark stretch of road. There was no sign of the snowmobile, but the truck's engine was loud enough to mask any sound of pursuit. She glanced back. The road was empty and still.

"Thanks," he said, taking the sharp curve easily.

"Where are we headed? Town?" Arden asked, pulling Sebastian out of the carrier and depositing him on her lap.

"Not Berlin. We'll need to stop for gas at some point, but we'll do it when we're farther away."

"You really are very good at avoiding my questions," she said.

He smiled. "We're going to Massachusetts. Cape Cod, to be specific."

Arden's heart jumped, her pulse racing. "You do realize GeoArray headquarters are in Boston, don't you?"

"Yes."

"And you want to go to Massachusetts because…?"

"It won't be expected, and because I have a cottage there."

"You have a cottage?"

"It belonged to my grandparents. They left it to me. I haven't been out to it in over a decade, but my parents use it in the summer, so it should be in decent shape."

"Decent shape for what?"

"Laying low until we can come up with a better plan."

She almost protested. She had no intention of

staying anywhere near GeoArray. She sure didn't plan on staying in a cottage with Kane. It was only a matter of time before someone linked Kane to that plane. Any property that could be traced to him would be the first place they'd search.

The words were on the tip of her tongue, but for once common sense won out. Until she had a better plan, she'd just have to go along for the ride. Let him think she was cooperating. It was becoming increasingly clear that giving him the slip was not going to be easy. Perhaps she should try another tactic. Get him on her side, then convince him that she'd be safer going off the grid again. Alone.

"You've gone quiet," Kane said. "You don't like the plan?"

"I'm tired." She sidestepped the question, and she was certain he noticed.

He didn't comment. Just turned up the heater that was blowing lukewarm air into the cab. He pulled the sopping knit cap from her head, his fingers brushing against her ear and the side of her neck.

He'd taken his gloves off at some point, and his fingers were warm and calloused against her cold skin.

"Go ahead and close your eyes for a while. We've got a long ride ahead of us, and you're probably going to want to work on those files once we reach the Cape."

She did want to work on the files, but she wasn't planning to rest now. She had too much on her mind and on her heart.

Juniper had trusted her to prove her husband's innocence and to clear his name. Arden had foolishly promised to do it. She'd had no idea what she was getting herself into, and she had no way of letting Juniper know what she'd learned. She also had no way of letting her friend know that she was safe.

"Juniper is probably worried sick," she murmured.

"So are Jace and Grayson. I'd put in a call to let them know you're with me, but the FBI is probably monitoring their cell phones."

"Right." She sighed, leaning her head back against the cracked leather seat and closing her eyes. Not because she planned to sleep, but because she didn't want to talk.

She was afraid everything would spill out. All her dramatic speculations about just how dangerous those files might be, about what they might be hiding, was better left unsaid. The less she told Kane, the better off he'd be. Two people were already dead because of those files. She was certain Juniper's husband had been murdered and that his boss had suffered the same fate.

She just had to prove it.

She had to decrypt those files.

Most of all, she had to make sure that whatever GeoArray had started was stopped.

And she'd really like to do it all before Christmas. She missed her family. She missed baking with her mother. She missed shopping with Juniper. She missed being home where she knew exactly what each day would bring.

She sniffed back unexpected tears, disgusted with herself. She wasn't a crier. She'd never been a crier. Even when she'd discovered the truth about Randy, she hadn't cried. She certainly wasn't going to cry now. She sniffed again, trying to prove that truth to herself.

"Are you crying?" Kane asked.

"Why would I be?" she asked, not opening her eyes. She was afraid a tear might slip out.

"Because you've been running for weeks? Because you're tired? Because it's almost Christmas and you're far from home?"

Yes. To all those things.

"I'm this close to decrypting those files, Kane. I just want to get somewhere where I can concentrate on doing it," she responded.

He didn't say anything. Just let the truck fill with their silence.

That was fine.

She was fine.

Or she would be. Once she fulfilled her promise to Juniper and made it back home.

Please, God, let that happen. Please, she

prayed silently, her eyes still closed as the truck descended the mountain.

They made it down the mountain in twenty minutes with no sign they were being followed. Kane fished his cell phone out of his pocket and dialed Silas. The call went directly to voice mail.

"Hey, it's me. I've got Jace's sister. The plane's down just outside of Berlin—I'll need you to handle it for me. We're headed to the Cape. Give me a call when you get this."

Another few hours, and they'd be at the Cape. Unfortunately.

He hoped he was making the right decision.

His name wasn't on the Cessna's title and hadn't been used to file the flight plan. The plane was owned by Shadow Wolves Security. They'd purposely not tied any of their names directly to the company to help maintain anonymity for the benefit of their clients. Discretion would be paramount to their future success.

It would be difficult for anyone to put his name together with Arden's but it wouldn't be impossible. If the FBI tied Kane's name to the company and the plane, they'd be able to quickly figure out that he owned the cottage.

A good reason to stay away, but he figured it would take time for the Feds to realize he and Arden were together. He could use that time to make plans.

For now, the Cape was his best option, but he didn't want to go there.

He'd left it almost thirteen years ago, and he hadn't looked back. There were too many memories, too many regrets.

He'd been a stupid punk when he'd spent summers and winter vacations there with his grandparents. His parents had never had time for more than a couple of days off during school break. They'd had busy lecture schedules that took them to many universities, hospitals and research facilities around the globe. None of those engagements would be considered fun for an active kid like Kane.

So when he wasn't in boarding school, he'd been shipped off to his grandparents at the Cape. Seventeen years of hanging out with the same spoiled summer crowd. Seventeen years of being Mr. Popular, Mr. Cool, Mr. Least-Likely-to-Get-Caught.

Seventeen years, then it all changed.

One bad decision. One stupid choice. One moment forever etched in his mind.

Like Kane, Evan had never forgiven himself for Lexi's death. The party had been his idea. They'd been distracted and it had cost Lexi her life. Two months later, Kane was left shouldering the guilt alone. Facing Evan's mom and siblings across another mahogany casket. Knowing he was one of the reasons they were grieving. There was no way he wanted to face Arden's family under similar circumstances.

He'd caused enough harm to last a lifetime. He'd enlisted in the army, both to honor Evan's plan to join the military and to atone for his role in Lexi's and Evan's deaths. Evan had intended to send money to his mom to help support his siblings. Instead, Kane did that for him. Every month. While in the army, Kane had found God. He'd been forgiven, but he'd never been able to forgive himself.

His hands tightened on the steering wheel, his heart pounding painfully.

That summer had altered the course of his life for the better. He knew that. But he'd still give anything to go back, to change what had happened, to make a different decision. He'd lived with those regrets for thirteen years. He definitely didn't need any more.

The drive into Cape Cod took longer than it should have. Sudden winds and icy snow hampered their progress along I-93. The blinding, relentless storm didn't let up for more than an hour.

Arden was silent for most of the four-hour ride. She'd handed him cash when he'd stopped in a small town to fill the tank, asked once how many miles stood between them and the Cape. Other than that, she didn't speak.

Though she'd dozed on and off, she'd stayed

awake for the majority of the trip. He felt her tension as he crept along the nearly empty highway. He hoped she wasn't planning her escape.

She could plan all she wanted, but she wasn't going to succeed. The more he knew about what she'd gotten herself into, the more dangerous it seemed. She needed help and protection. Whether she wanted to admit it or not.

"We'll be at the cottage in less than ten minutes," he said quietly, and she opened her eyes, straightening in her seat and stretching a kink in her neck. Sebastian protested as she disturbed his sleep.

"Silly boy," she said, patting the cat's fuzzy head. "I'm sorry I woke you. Just a little while longer and you'll be able to freely roam about for a bit."

"He's been a pretty good traveling companion."

"Running-for-our-lives companion is more like it. I should have left him at home, but I'd have had to ask someone to watch him, and that would have meant explaining why I needed to leave. Plus, he'd have missed me."

"And you'd have missed him?"

"Of course. Aside from my dad and brothers, he's the only guy who's ever been loyal to me." She must have realized what she said. "What I mean is, he and I have been buddies for a long time."

"Randy isn't loyal?" he asked, not really surprised and not really disappointed that she must have finally seen the guy for what he was. Kane had met him a couple of times, and that had been a couple of times too many. The guy was an arrogant blowhard who seemed to get a kick out of poking fun at Arden. All Arden's brothers had thought the same.

"He's not part of my life anymore, so how about we change the subject?"

"To?"

"The weather seems like a safe choice. The storm is breaking. It should be a good night for coding."

"Or sleeping," he suggested.

"I'm too wound up, and I'm way too close to accessing what's in those files."

She leaned her forehead against the window as they crawled through town. The roads were lightly layered with snow, the businesses decorated for the season with bright lights, wreaths and ribbon. "I've never been to Cape Cod, but I like it. They know how to do Christmas right."

"So there's a way to do that?"

"Sure." She pointed at several pine trees decorated with colored lights and red bows. "That's the right way. Bright. Fun. Happy."

"I'll take your word for it."

"You're not a Grinch are you?"

"What?"

"A Scrooge? A Christmas curmudgeon?"

"I like Christmas as much as the next person,"

he said, turning onto a side road that would bring them closer to the beach.

"You don't sound very enthusiastic about it."

"My family never made that big of a deal about the holidays."

"No big family celebrations when you were a kid?"

"I mostly celebrated with my grandparents. It was nice. Quiet. A good meal and a couple of gifts." And parents who'd called around noon to ask if he liked whatever they'd given him.

Kane could only remember one or two times that his parents had been home during the holidays. Even then, they'd shipped him to his grandparents during his school breaks and joined him on Christmas Day.

"That sounds…lonely."

"It wasn't. I always had a good time. My grandparents were great."

"Did they raise you?"

"Mostly. What they didn't do, boarding school took care of. My parents were busy."

"Doing what?"

"Being internationally renowned geneticists. They spent a lot of time traveling to hospitals, labs and universities." He turned onto Sea Street and followed it to the end. His grandparents' 1835 cottage sat on two acres there. Surrounded by tall evergreen trees on three sides, it was bordered on the fourth by a sandy section of beach. He'd spent a lot of time there. He thought he knew it and re-membered it well, but it looked different now—the cottage more quaint than he remembered, the yard larger.

"Is this it?" Arden asked as he pulled into the snow-covered drive.

"Yes."

"It's cute. It would be even cuter with some Christmas lights, a Nativity scene, a wreath."

He followed the driveway around to the back of the house, driving under the boughs of an over-grown spruce. Everything was locked up for the winter. His parents used the place a few times a year. Usually in the summer and spring. Other than that, it stayed empty, the skeleton key that opened the back door hidden in a faux rock that sat at the edge of the flower bed.

He pulled up to the detached garage. A motion-activated light above the garage door flicked on and illuminated the area. There were no footprints in the pristine snow, no tire tracks on the paved drive. Kane cut the engine.

"Here's how it's going to go," he said, reach-ing over the seat and grabbing Arden's back-pack. "We'll go in the back door. You'll stay in the house. I'll get the key for the garage and move the truck into it."

"Okay," she responded.

"You're agreeing that easily?" he asked. He eyed the back of the cottage. His grandmother's gnome was still standing guard in the barren flower bed. Beside it, the cement birdbath stood empty. The place had an air of neglect that bothered him. Sure, it was still charming but in a few years, it would look like so many forgotten properties—lonely and old.

"Of course. I've got work to do, remember?"

He remembered. He also remembered that she didn't want to go back to her family. She didn't want other people involved in her trouble, and she'd been wanting to lose him since the moment he'd found her.

He grabbed his duffel as well, and got out of the truck, listening to the winter silence. Cape Cod was busy in the summer, but this time of year, it quieted down. Mostly locals and a few die-hard visitors who loved the beach in the winter.

"It's quiet," Arden whispered as she climbed out of the truck, Sebastian in her arms.

"The quieter the better," he responded. He put a hand on her back and urged her to the rear stoop. He stopped at the flower bed, lifting the rock his grandfather had bought decades ago. His grandmother used to constantly lock herself out of the house.

Thinking about what a great couple they'd been, how committed to each other and to their only daughter and to him, made him smile.

"Are you planning to break a window?" Arden asked, eyeing the rock as he turned it over in his hand. The compartment that housed the key opened easily, and he dumped the key into his palm.

"Not unless this key doesn't do its job."

"I hope it does. It's freezing out here."

"I can't promise it'll be any warmer in the house." He shoved the key into the lock and turned it. He opened the door and held it so that Arden could walk into the mudroom at the back of the house.

He followed her inside, pulling the door closed and turning the lock. The mudroom was small, the kitchen just beyond it pitch-black. He expected the place to have the closed-up musty smell of a house that hadn't been used in a while, but it smelled like...

Christmas?

Cinnamon for sure.

Pine.

Something else that he couldn't quite place. Cookies maybe. Or bread.

Whatever it was, it didn't belong. He grabbed Arden's arm, pulling her back.

"Something isn't right," he muttered, the hair on his nape standing on end. "We need to get out of here."

Too late.

A floorboard creaked and the kitchen light flicked on.

Kane stepped between Arden and the threat, dropping her pack and pulling his gun in one quick movement.

TEN

Arden had always wondered if a person's heart could actually stop from fear.

Now she knew.

It could.

Hers had.

It started again when a woman screamed, the high-pitched sound like a jolt of electricity to Arden's flagging cardiac muscle. Arden jumped, her grip on Sebastian loosening. Sebastian yowled and twisted out of her arms.

Arden grabbed for him. Missed. Started after him as he rushed across the room.

"Sebastian!" she yelled, her heart pounding over the sound of other voices.

"Stop!" Kane commanded, and Sebastian did, plopping his furry body down on a pretty throw rug near the kitchen sink. Arden skidded to a standstill a couple of inches from Sebastian.

"What in the world," a woman said, "is going on here?"

Arden whirled around, found herself three feet from an older couple. Flannel pajamas, bare feet, salt-and-pepper hair. They were a matched set. The man clutched a baseball bat. The woman held a huge tome that probably outweighed her by several pounds.

"Is that *The Iliad*?" Arden asked, and the woman glanced down at the book.

"Why, yes! It is," she responded.

"Light reading before bed, Mom?" Kane asked, slipping his gun back into the holster beneath his coat.

"Mom?" Arden repeated, but no one seemed all that interested in responding.

"This was one of your grandfather's books. It was the first thing I could find that could be used as a weapon." The woman set the book down on the counter. "We were certain we were about to get murdered in our beds."

"Except that we're not in our beds, dear," the man pointed out. He leaned the baseball bat against the wall and let it rest there. "We would have been murdered in the kitchen. It's good to see you, son. It's surprising, but good."

"I'm as surprised as you are." Kane ran a hand over his hair. "I thought you were overseas."

"We flew back a few days ago," the woman said, her gaze darting to Arden. "We got to our place and a pipe had burst. They're fixing it and drying everything out, so we decided to stay here until the work was finished. You did say that we could use the cottage any time."

"Right. I did."

"So…" Arden cut into what seemed like an awfully awkward conversation. Shouldn't they be hugging? Throwing themselves into each other's arms and talking about how much they'd missed each other? "I guess these are your parents?"

"Julia and Henry Walker," Kane said. "Mom and Dad, this is Arden DeMarco."

"DeMarco…" Mr. Walker mused. "Why do I know that name?"

"Because my business partner is Jace DeMarco, Arden's…"

"No, no. That's not it," Mrs. Walker interjected. "Remember, Henry? That paper we read on quantum computing?"

"Oh, that's right! Superb work. Real cutting-edge stuff." Mr. Walker smiled broadly. "Are you *that* Arden DeMarco?"

"Yes," she admitted, surprised that they'd read any of her work. "It was part of my dissertation."

"Your theory on error-correction algorithms was groundbreaking. Were you really able to use only four qubits?"

"To a point," Arden answered. "Unfortunately, as you are probably aware, interference is still an issue, even with the use of trapped ion qubits with intense magnetic fields."

"So true, yet the technology is promising," Mrs. Walker added, smoothing her hair and smiling at her son. "Kane, we're infringing on your time with your *friend*. Your father and I will pack our things and go to a hotel."

"Why would we do that? This place is plenty big enough for all of us, and I want to talk to Arden about her research," Mr. Walker said.

"As do I, but I think that Arden and Kane would prefer to talk to each other."

"Statistically speaking, after traveling here together, they are probably both ready for a break from each other. Why, just yesterday, I read a study on couples. Genetics aside, we tend to be attracted to that which is both different and familiar." Mr. Walker was off chasing rabbits, and Arden had a moment of clarity, a moment of absolute vivid truth—Kane's parents? They were her flannel-clad, tome-carrying people.

"Wow," she breathed, and Kane grinned. He took her elbow and led her through the kitchen and out into a cozy living room.

"I figured you'd like them," he murmured, his lips so close to her ear that she could feel the warmth of his breath.

"I like you, too," she responded, the words out before she could stop them. Her cheeks were suddenly hot. "What I mean—"

"Don't ruin the moment," he replied, smiling.

And she couldn't make herself say what she'd been going to. Not while she was looking into his gold-flecked eyes, seeing the humor there.

"How far did you two travel today? Miles or kilometers is fine," Mrs. Walker said.

"Longer than either of us planned to, Mrs. Walker," Arden said. As much as she loved talking shop and chasing intellectual rabbits, she was more interested in decrypting files, finding her answers and shutting down GeoArray. "I'm exhausted," she added. Just in case the older woman hadn't gotten the hint.

"Call me Jules. And my husband answers to Henry. Your father and I are in the room at the top of the stairs, Kane. That leaves the blue room and the yellow."

"Let's give Arden the yellow," Kane said.

"It *is* the larger of the two." Henry stepped into the room, Arden's backpack over his shoulders, Sebastian cradled in his arms. "My son has always been a gentleman. Is that one of the things that attracted you to him?"

"We're not—"

"Henry! What a thing to ask!"

"It's a valid question, honey. Remember that piece we read two months ago?" Henry started upstairs, continuing on about the article as he went. Jules followed, the two of them batting around statistics.

Henry disappeared into a room down a wide hallway and reappeared at the top of the stairs seconds later without Sebastian or the backpack.

"Do you need me to grab luggage from your car?" he asked.

Kane shook his head. "I'll take care of it."

"Then I'll head to bed. You know how I've always been. Early to bed and early to rise. Statistically speaking, people who live by that pattern have longer, healthier lives." Henry offered them a quick smile and went into his room.

"I really need to turn in, too," Jules said. "The bathroom is at the end of the hall, Arden. Linen closet is stocked with toiletries if you forgot anything."

She'd *forgotten* everything.

She couldn't tell Jules that, so she just nodded and smiled and said good-night. She followed Kane up the stairs, past the Walkers' bedroom door to her own room. The room was large, with a full-size bed, dresser, single nightstand and one window facing the front of the house.

It was definitely called the yellow room for a reason. Pale yellow walls and white bedding with yellow and orange flowers and throw pillows screamed of an era long gone. A yellow area rug under the bed covered most of the scratched wood floor.

She sat on the bed. "The room's been aptly named."

Kane stood at the threshold of the room, watching as she pulled her laptop from the backpack that Henry had left on the bed.

"It lacks a yellow brick road, but I hope it will do."

She laughed. "Well, there's no place like home, but this does have a homey feel."

He smiled. "My parents being here complicates things."

"Should we leave?"

"We're both running on fumes, so it's best if we stay, at least for the night. Hopefully, they won't call the neighbors to brag about their houseguest and her dissertation work."

She laughed and flicked on her computer. Her mind was already sprinting ahead, working through the files. She wouldn't work yet, though.

Kane was correct—his parents being in the house added a whole new dimension to the problem. She definitely did not want them pulled into the mess she was in. There was no time to convince Kane to let her walk away. But this cottage just might offer her an unexpected chance to give Kane the slip. She'd let him think she was working, let him get settled in. Once he was asleep, she'd take Sebastian and go.

It was safer for everyone that way.

"You laugh, but the guy who lives at the end of the street is an astrophysicist. He'd love to meet you, and my parents would love to be the ones to make the introduction."

"I'm sure they mean well."

"They do, but we need to be as unobtrusive as possible."

"You do realize they think we're dating, don't you?" Arden asked.

"Yes. There's no sense arguing with them. They hear what they want to hear, especially at two in the morning." Kane gave her an easy smile and leaned against the doorframe.

Tall and muscular, he exuded confidence, affability and strength. They were a winning combination, and if she let herself, she could imagine seeing him at her family's Christmas celebration again this year. Instead of pretending to hang on every word Randy spoke, she'd be doing her own thing, free to talk to whomever she wanted.

"You're staring," he said. His hair was just long enough to curl at his nape, his eyes a light brown that looked almost gold in the soft yellow light.

"Sorry. I was zoning out." And being an idiot. Kane probably dated models and actresses and NFL cheerleaders. Not geeky computer experts.

"It's been a long day. A little zoning out is to be expected."

"A long couple of weeks," she admitted.

"Things will get easier from here. My associate, Silas Blackwater, can help us with GeoArray. I've already asked him to handle the plane."

"Teamwork is great, but this part—" she tapped her computer keyboard "—is something only I can do."

"Why you?" he asked, and she realized she'd said too much.

"I've been doing this for years," she hedged. She focused on the still-blank screen and pretended to type.

"You obviously aren't working, Arden. And you obviously aren't telling the truth."

"I *have* been doing this for years."

"Lots of people work in computer forensics. Lots of people know how to decrypt files. If you turned the files over to the FBI, they could put a team of people on it. It seems like that might be more effective. What is it about this encryption that makes it so difficult?" He sounded angry. She couldn't blame him. He'd risked his life for her, and she was withholding information from him.

His eyes never left hers as he waited for her response, the silence in the air heavy between them.

"It's complicated," she began, still hesitant to let him in.

"Try me."

"Aside from the person who encrypted the files, there's likely no one who can decrypt them as quickly as I'll be able to."

"Okay, I'll take the bait—why?"

"Because I developed the base encryption code that's wrapped around the files." She saw the surprise register in his eyes. Wished she could stop his next question before he said it.

"How did your code end up around those files?"

There it was. She could either lie or let him in on what a sham her relationship with Randy had been. As mortifying as the truth was, she couldn't bring herself to lie to him. Randy had used her. The facts were the facts. There was no use sugarcoating it. "Because when Randy and I worked at the university together, he had access to my research, stole my code, then passed it off as his own."

"Your boyfriend?"

"*Ex*-boyfriend," she corrected.

"Does he work for GeoArray?"

"He's apparently a consultant for them now. A very highly paid consultant."

"Which probably means they're willing to pay a hefty price to ensure the security of those files."

"Exactly," Arden agreed. "I think those files are somehow connected with GeoArray's one-hundred-dred-million-dollar contract to design and build a self-improving weapons command and control prototype."

"Self-improving?"

"In the loose sense of the word, it means artificial intelligence or machine learning."

"I thought that was mostly academic conjecture?"

"It has been, but inroads have been made lately. For instance, in credit card fraud recognition programs. The concepts are definitely becoming more mainstream."

"So this application will do what?"

"Without getting my hands on the research, I can't know for sure, but there are numerous possibilities. It could be programmed to learn if-then scenarios to have weapons change course after launch based on real-time data."

"So that means a nuclear missile, for instance, could be made to abort or self-detonate?"

"Yes. It could even change targets on its own based on the programmed scenarios."

"That could be catastrophic."

"I agree—a system like that could turn one of our weapons against an ally or ourselves."

"Do you think they may be close to completing the application?"

"The government picked up the contract's option years last October without recompeting it—" she stifled a yawn "—so there's a pretty good chance that's the case."

"You're probably right." Kane straightened. "But maybe you should think about getting some rest tonight. Start fresh in the morning. You might have better results."

"I won't work too long. I just want to try something I've been thinking about," she said.

He started to leave, but turned back. "Remember, we're in this together now. You worry about decrypting those files and I'll take care of everything else."

"Got it," she said to his back as he closed the

bedroom door behind him. Kane said all the right things, but she knew what she had to do. In the long run, everyone would be safer once she dropped off the grid again.

She was going to try to leave.

There was absolutely no doubt in Kane's mind about that.

He was going to stop her. There was no doubt about that, either. Whether or not she'd still like him when it was over? That was something that remained to be seen.

He jogged downstairs, grabbing the keys to the garage from the hook near the front door. His grandfather had made a habit of putting the keys there to help his grandmother. She'd always been forgetful, but things had been worse during the last decade of her life.

I can't have my best friend feeling bad about forgetting, so let's make it easier for her to remember.

Kane could almost hear his grandfather's words ringing through the quiet house. They'd been a team, putting up the key hooks, purchasing a high-tech oven that turned itself off if left on for too long.

He'd not thought much of it then, but looking back on it he could see that those times with his grandparents had shaped the man he would become. It was fact that he'd spent the first seventeen years of his life running after acceptance and popularity and fun. But that summer before his senior year had changed all that.

It had been a typical Friday night. Evan was stuck watching his siblings while his mom worked a second job. Kane insisted a party would be a good idea. By the time they'd found Lexi in the pool, it was too late.

That decision haunted him. Now he chased after things that had meaning and eternal value. But Kane had long ago resigned himself to the fact that he'd likely never find that one person who would fill his heart with joy.

I like you, Kane, Arden had said. For some reason, that meant more to him than any compliment he'd ever received from any woman he'd ever dated.

Maybe because she'd said it without any desire for reciprocation. She hadn't asked for a response. She hadn't seemed to even want one. She'd simply been stating another one of her facts.

He frowned, stepping outside and letting the cold, crisp air fill his lungs. He could smell the ocean in it, the briny water and moist air. He'd always loved this place. Even tainted by the memories of what he'd done, it felt more like home than any other place ever had.

He crossed the yard and unlocked the two-bay garage. His parents' car was on the left. The right bay was empty, his grandparents' old Chrysler long gone. He pulled the truck into place, then took out his cell phone and tried to reach Silas again.

This time Silas picked up.

"Silas, we've got a problem." Kane explained Arden's theory as succinctly as he could. If what Arden believed was true, keeping her safe while she decrypted the files had become more than just a personal mission. It was a matter of national security. As was his way, Silas listened without commenting, until Kane was through.

After they discussed their next move, Kane hung up, satisfied backup was on its way. He'd have called Grayson, but that was too dangerous. He couldn't risk his call being intercepted by the Feds. He'd promised Arden the time she needed to decrypt those files.

He tucked the phone into his pocket, got out of the truck and closed the garage door.

One less thing to worry about.

A few dozen more to take care of.

Like his parents.

He glanced up at the cottage, eyeing the window of their room. No light, and he assumed they'd done what they'd said they would and gone to bed.

Tomorrow morning would be soon enough to ask them to keep quiet about his "girlfriend." Hopefully, they'd cooperate.

Hopefully, they wouldn't ask a million questions.

He didn't want to lie, but there was no way he could tell them the truth without endangering them.

He did a perimeter check of the property, the velvety silence of the early morning enveloping him. No sign of movement on the street in front of the house. Nothing to the rear. No lights. No vehicles. There was no reason to believe they'd been found, and every reason to believe they would be eventually.

Their time was limited by that, and by whatever was in those files.

He reached the area of the cottage beneath Arden's window. She'd turned off her light. Maybe she thought that he'd assume she was asleep. Maybe she just hoped it.

No sense making her wait too long to try her escape.

He went back inside and walked up the steps loudly enough for her to hear. Opened and closed the door to his room with just enough force to be convincing.

Once the sounds settled into quiet, he walked back downstairs, avoiding the creaky tread on the third and fifth steps, the groaning floorboard near the kitchen. He pulled a chair away from the table where he'd once eaten breakfast, lunch and dinner with his grandparents and sat, waiting for Arden to make her move.

ELEVEN

Arden's eyes drifted shut for what seemed like the fifteenth time in as many minutes. She forced them open again and got to her feet. It was now or never. If she didn't make her escape, she'd accidentally fall asleep and lose the opportunity.

She strapped on Sebastian's carrier, then slipped into her coat. Shrugging the straps of the pack onto her shoulders, she glanced at the antique clock sitting on the dresser. Nearly three in the morning. The house had been quiet for almost an hour.

Time to go, but she really didn't want to.

Being part of a team working to take down GeoArray seemed so much easier than going it alone. But Kane's parents were now in the equation. Two people were already dead. She couldn't risk more lives.

Arden plucked Sebastian from his cozy spot between the pillows and deposited him in the carrier.

She crossed the room in darkness, cracked open the door. Head cocked, she strained to hear signs that her movement had disturbed anyone. Hearing nothing, she stepped into the hallway, keeping close to the walls and praying she could avoid the groans and creaks from the old, worn floor.

At the top of the stairwell, she paused and peered down into the darkness below. With Kane's room toward the rear of the house, the front door gave her the highest probability of slipping out unheard. Of course, once she got the truck started, he'd wake up.

If she got it started.

She'd read about hot-wiring cars. So she had all the steps memorized, but she'd never done it.

She crept silently down the steps, crossed the foyer and fumbled with the lock on the front door. Turning the handle, she slowly eased the door open and looked out into the dark morning. It would be hours before the sun rose. That gave her time to make her way back through town and out onto the interstate again before the town woke. The less people who knew she'd been there, the safer it would be for Kane's parents.

She'd find a place somewhere far away, she'd decrypt the files, and then she'd pass the information to Grayson and let him take it from there.

First, though, she had to get the truck started.

She scanned the yard and the street beyond it. Everything looked just like it had when they'd arrived—pristine snow blanketing grass and driveway. Across the street, a pretty little cottage was tucked away from the road, the lights off, the driveway empty. There was an SUV parked on the street in front of it. Had it been there when they'd arrived?

She couldn't remember seeing any vehicles on the street, but she'd been tired and distracted. She leaned farther out the door, staring hard at the SUV and the shadowed driver's window.

Was someone in there?

The vehicle's door swung open and a man got out. He stood near the driver's door, looking in her direction.

There were no streetlights, no moonglow, nothing to illuminate his face or eyes. But she was absolutely sure he was looking right at her. And she was absolutely positive he was about to head her way.

He took the first step, and she jumped back into the house, knocking into something firm and warm.

A hand slammed over her mouth.

She screamed.

Or tried. All that came out was a muffled squeak. An arm slid around her waist, and Sebastian—traitor that he was—started purring.

"Not a good idea, Arden," Kane said quietly.

Because, of course, it was Kane.

He'd set her up. He'd known she was going to try to leave, and he'd given her the opportunity.

She shoved his hand away, whirling to face him. Angry that he'd made her look like a fool. Terrified that guy who'd been crossing the street was still coming.

"There's someone out there," she managed to say, her voice shaking with emotion.

"I know," he said simply. "That's Silas Blackwater. He's Jace's and my business partner."

"You could have warned me about him before I opened the door. It would have saved my heart some effort," she snapped, and he frowned.

"You're angry."

"Of course I am. You made a fool out of me." She *was* angry. She'd lost count of the number of times Randy had made her feel the fool. "You pretended you believed me, made a big show about your nighttime routine, then sneaked down here and basically lay in wait for me when all you needed to do was—"

"Stop," he interrupted, pressing three fingers gently to her lips. "First of all, I only found out an hour ago that Silas decided to head to the Cape rather than New Hampshire. Second, it would be impossible to make you look like a fool. You're too intelligent to ever be mistaken for one." He dropped his hand from her mouth, stepped closer and removed Sebastian from his carrier. The little Judas purred loudly as Kane scratched behind his ears.

"And lastly, I didn't tell you I was onto you because that wouldn't have stopped you from hatching your next plan. You're too determined. You know what you're up against and you don't want to put anyone else in danger. Not Juniper, my parents or me. That's one of the things I admire about you. But I needed you to understand that you won't be able to slip away from me. We're in this together. Whether you like it or not."

He set Sebastian on the floor. The cat wove between her legs, then Kane's, before climbing the stairs toward the yellow room without so much as a backward glance.

Arden's anger started to melt away. He'd just spent an entire night up close and personal with all her little foibles, yet he thought it would be impossible for her to look like a fool?

The door clicked shut softly behind her. Arden whirled around with a startled yelp and found herself face to chest with Kane's associate, his arms laden with kitty litter and a plastic shopping bag brimming with supplies. She was touched by Kane's thoughtfulness.

She took a step back, looked up into a pair of heavy-lidded green eyes. He was easily over six feet tall with straight black hair tied in a short, low ponytail. Lean and muscular, his swarthy skin, high cheekbones and aquiline nose all spoke to his Native American heritage.

"Sorry, I didn't hear you come up behind me," Arden said.

"You weren't supposed to," he said simply.

"This is Silas Blackwater. He's with us from

now on." Kane's tone left no room for argument. He reached around Arden and took the shopping bag from Silas. "Now let's come up with a plan of action we can all agree on." He turned toward the kitchen, clearly expecting Arden to follow. With Silas behind her blocking the front door, she didn't have much choice.

If she was honest with herself, she was warming up to the idea of being part of a team. Maybe it was time she stopped relying on herself and started taking advantage of the resources God placed in front of her. And she couldn't deny that Kane made her feel safe. Like it was okay for her to be her. Like he wouldn't have it any other way.

She shrugged out of her pack and followed Kane into the kitchen. She'd give the whole team thing a shot, but first she needed to break the code that protected those files, and that was something she'd have to do alone.

Kane placed the bag on the table and started unloading the supplies. In addition to a plastic litter pan and a bag of cat food, he'd asked Silas to bring some breakfast food. He was pretty sure Arden must be starved. He knew he was. Kane pulled the last item from the bag, held it up and looked at Silas. "Hershey's Kisses?"

"Don't all girls like chocolate?" Silas shrugged.

"This one does," Arden piped up, snatching the bag of assorted chocolate kisses from Kane's hand and ripping into it. "And I can definitely use the sugar right about now." She popped one in her mouth. "Mmm. So good. Thanks, Silas."

"No problem." Silas had the decency not to gloat as he placed the box of kitty litter on the floor. "Dutch is in the yard taking care of business," he said, walking toward the back door. "Do you mind if I let him in?"

"Go for it," Kane responded.

"Dutch?" Arden booted up her laptop and reached for another chocolate.

"My dog." Silas opened the back door and gave a piercing whistle. "He served in combat with us."

"He's retired?" Arden asked, typing on her keyboard.

"By default," Kane explained. "When Silas decided to get out, Dutch was supposed to be placed with another handler, but no one could get the Sioux commands quite right."

"At least that's the theory." Silas grinned. Dutch crossed the threshold into the kitchen. Silas shut the door behind him.

"Are you sure he's a dog?" Arden pulled her earbuds from her bag, eyeing Dutch from her seat at the kitchen table.

"He's a Czechoslovakian Wolfdog, to be exact." Silas gave a command in Sioux. The dog immediately lay on the rug by the back door.

"Looks like more wolf than dog to me," Arden mused before shoving the earbuds into her ears.

"The chocolate's given me a renewed burst of energy. I'm going to see if I can get this algorithm working before dawn."

"I'm not sure if my parents had time to call and get the Wi-Fi switched on yet, but you can use my cell phone as a hot spot if you'd like."

"The Wi-Fi's active," she responded, popping another chocolate into her mouth.

"Great, let me know if you need the password for it," Kane said.

"No need. I'm in already."

"How'd you get around the password?"

She met his eyes across the table. "Have you forgotten what I do for a living?"

Silas snickered.

"I just didn't realize you could hack in so quickly. You've only been sitting there for a few minutes."

"It's a known fact that people tend to choose passwords that are easy to remember and mean something to them. In this case, your last name, the word *home* and the house number were used. You should probably consider changing it."

"I'll do that," Kane responded drily, but Arden didn't seem to hear him. She was lost in her work, her jet-black, shoulder-length hair tucked casually behind her ear, thick-lashed eyes focused on the screen in front of her.

She was the exact opposite of every woman that had even remotely attracted him in the past, but he found himself drawn to her. She was extremely intelligent, but that was only part of the person she was.

Truth be told, she drew him in from the first time he met her, but his friendship with Jace and Arden's ever-present jerk of a boyfriend gave him plenty of reasons to tamp those feelings down. One of those reasons was now out of the picture. His friendship with Jace, on the other hand, would not be easy to get around.

Jace knew Kane before he became a Christian. He'd accepted him for all his past mistakes and helped him find his faith. But that didn't mean Jace would ever see Kane as good enough for his little sister. Kane wouldn't blame him there.

A rapid succession of buzzing tones came from Arden's laptop.

"That didn't sound promising," Kane commented.

"It's not great news, but on the plus side, I got past the first level of encryption. It's only a matter of time before I break the last."

He admired her confidence.

Nearly an hour later, Kane had filled Silas in on the events of the evening while making some breakfast sandwiches. Arden had scarfed down her food with a quick thanks, barely taking her eyes from the computer screen. Kane wondered about the progress she was making but didn't want to distract her from her task.

"Yes! Thank You, God!" Arden exclaimed happily.

"What?" Kane and Silas both came around the table and peered over her shoulder.

"My decryption application is loaded and ready to test." She stretched her arms and yawned. "We'll know in a few moments if it works." Her fingers ran over the keyboard. "Here goes nothing," she said and pressed Enter to launch the program.

"Is it working?" Silas asked.

"Yes. Yes. Yes!"

Kane tried to focus on the rows of code that scrolled quickly across the dark screen. He had no idea what he was looking at, but judging by her enthusiasm, he predicted success. "How long will it take to run?"

"It's almost complete." As if on cue, a tune erupted from the computer—a tune that sounded suspiciously like the fanfare in one of his retro video games that signaled a player had found an important item. Typical Arden. Kane couldn't help but smile.

Arden pulled up the first of the decrypted files and began reading. Kane and Silas attempted to read over her shoulder.

"I can't keep up. She's reading way too fast," Silas commented.

"I'm in the same boat," Kane said, still trying to skim the contents of the files as Arden clicked from page to page.

"Houston, we have a problem." Arden focused on the screen in front of her, still scrolling through documents.

"What is it?" Kane asked.

"Oh, no," she said flatly. She leveled her gaze on him and shut her laptop. "It's worse than I thought. Marcus Emory is not just selling research—he's planning to sell the code for the prototype of the self-improving weapons control program that GeoArray developed for the Department of Defense."

"To who?" Kane asked.

"It's not clear, but my guess is it's a foreign buyer. The first payment was wired to an offshore account about a month ago. The rest will be paid on delivery of the weapons control system. The trade is scheduled for two days from now. We don't have much time."

Kane thought Arden was probably spot-on. She'd been right to this point, so it was likely Marcus Emory was planning to sell United States secrets to the highest bidder. Likely a nation-state entity that could threaten world peace.

A low growl sounded from the corner. Dutch was standing alert by the back door. "Someone's out there," Silas whispered.

"Let's check it out."

Arden started to get up from the table.

"You stay here, Arden, and keep away from the windows," Kane said. "Silas and I will handle this."

For a moment, Arden looked ready to argue the point, but Kane decided to beat her to the punch. "Someone needs to remain here and be ready to warn my parents if needed."

"You're right, of course." She sat back down, began to pack her computer. "But just be careful."

Kane and Silas left through the front door.

"You take the left and I'll take the right." Kane was only slightly mollified by Arden's promise to stay put. He'd hated to leave her alone in the kitchen, but nothing else could be done.

Silas headed toward the front corner of the house, Dutch at his heels. Kane didn't bother to warn him to keep quiet. If Silas didn't want you to hear him coming, you wouldn't.

Kane saw fresh footprints in the snow leading to the back of the house. Someone was here.

He slipped around the corner, saw a shadowy figure advancing toward the kitchen window, something dark in his hand. A gun?

Kane rushed forward and tackled him, the impact sending them both reeling into the side of the house. Something black fell from the man's hand. Kane jumped up and grabbed for it. A tactical flashlight? Oh, boy.

Within seconds, Silas and Dutch were at his side. Kane shined his light on the man who was still sprawled facedown in the snow.

Silas turned him over. Snow coated the man's uniform and stuck to his face. "You just knocked out a cop, bro."

Kane looked at the nametag on the man's department-issued jacket. Deputy C. Moran. Great.

"Deputy Moran, this is dispatch. Please report findings from the Walker place. Over." A woman's voice crackled through the radio holstered to the officer's belt. Kane looked at Silas, whose expression likely mirrored Kane's thoughts. Not good. "Deputy Moran, do you copy? Over."

"We need to get your girl and book it before dispatch sends backup. I'm guessing that the local cops are checking out the place as a favor to the FBI. It probably won't be long before either Geo-Array or the FBI show up."

Kane had been thinking the same thing. The FBI had somehow connected him to the plane. The Cape was no longer safe for any of them. He handed the flashlight to Silas and hoisted the deputy on his shoulder.

"What are we going to do with him?"

"I haven't thought that far ahead, but we can't just leave him here in below-freezing temperatures. Let's get him to the house."

TWELVE

Three minutes, ten seconds.

Three minutes, eleven seconds.

Arden watched the second hand on the old grandmother clock creep to twelve, thirteen, fourteen.

Every second seemed like an eternity. Every minute that passed brought them closer to disaster. Someone had been outside. Silas's dog had made that clear. If it were one of GeoArray's thugs, there'd be more assassins waiting in the shadows.

She shuddered, sliding the laptop back in her pack. Now she understood why GeoArray had been so desperate to retrieve the files and stop her from opening them.

She understood, and it terrified her.

There had to be a way to keep them from releasing the information, and she planned to find it. Standing around waiting for Kane and Silas to return wasn't helping her do that.

Besides, she wasn't just terrified. She was worried.

Logically, she knew that Kane and Silas didn't

need her help, but logic had nothing to do with the heart. And her heart was telling her they might be in trouble, that even with all their combined training and expertise, they might have run into a situation they couldn't get out of.

She grabbed the baseball bat that Henry had abandoned earlier and walked to the back door. She peered out the little window beside it.

The light above the garage door was still glowing, illuminating footprints and tire tracks left in the snow. A shadow moved near the corner of the garage, and a man appeared. Tall. Broad shoulders. Moving toward the house, a dog beside him.

Silas. It had to be. The dog wouldn't be walking beside anyone else.

She unlocked the door and stepped onto the back stoop, still clutching the baseball bat.

"Where's Kane?" she asked, and Silas gestured toward the back corner of the house.

"Coming. You need to get your things. We need to move out."

"My things are ready to go." She stepped back as he walked up the steps, crowding into her space and making no apology for it.

"Go back inside, Arden. It isn't safe out here."

"Did you find the person who was out there?" she asked, peering around him and finally catching a glimpse of Kane.

He was moving across the yard, something

flung over his shoulder. A bag of some sort? An animal?

The closer he got, the more it looked like…

A person?

"In the house," Silas repeated, and somehow he had her moving backward, across the threshold and into the mudroom.

Once she was inside, he moved past her, the dog trotting along beside him.

Seconds later, Kane appeared in the doorway.

"You were supposed to stay inside," he growled. He closed the door with a little more force than she thought was necessary.

"Shh!" she cautioned. "You're going to wake up your parents."

"You were supposed to stay inside," he repeated, his eyes flashing with irritation as he strode past. The person he was carrying hung limply over his shoulder.

A man.

She could see that now.

In a police uniform.

"Is he dead?" she asked as Kane set the guy in a chair.

"No." Kane's response was terse. He grabbed Arden's backpack and was sliding into it. "Did you leave anything upstairs?"

"Just Sebastian. I'll get him. He's not going to be happy when I put him back in the carrier. I think he's sick of traveling. Cats aren't known for being fond of it. I read an interesting article about—"

The floorboards in front of the kitchen doorway creaked, cutting off the rest of whatever babbling diatribe Arden had been about to deliver.

Nerves.

Because she knew Kane was upset, because there was an unconscious police officer in a chair at the kitchen table, because everything was riding on them being able to stop GeoArray before the company transferred the system to a buyer and she was scared they wouldn't get the opportunity.

"What's going on?" Henry asked, walking into the kitchen. Jules was right behind him. "Why is Chuck Moran here?" His focus jumped from the officer to Silas. "And who are you?"

"Silas is my business associate," Kane explained, taking the baseball bat from Arden's hand and setting it on the table. "The officer ran into some trouble."

"What kind of trouble?" Jules hurried across the room, lifting the officer's wrist and checking his pulse.

"He was outside the house. I thought he was trying to break in. I knocked him out before I realized he was law enforcement."

"Did you also think he had something to do with whatever Arden has gotten herself involved in?" Jules asked.

Arden met Kane's eyes. He looked as surprised as she felt.

"What are you talking about, Mom?" he asked.

"Arden was on the evening news last night. That's one of the reasons why Henry and I remembered that article so well. Right, honey?" She plugged in the coffeepot and filled the reservoir.

"Right. They even had a picture of you, Arden. Apparently, the FBI has you on its most wanted list. Someone spotted you at an airport in Maine. I heard your name and remembered you from that article, so I looked it up online to refresh my memory. Very interesting read, Arden. Very interesting."

"Why," Kane began, and Arden thought he was doing everything in his power to hold onto his patience, "was the local evening news running a story about Arden, Dad?"

"It was a short piece, really. Simply said the FBI believed Arden to be traveling with an unknown male companion and that they were likely headed toward Massachusetts and one or both could be armed. Once you showed up here, we realized that the FBI was totally wrong about whatever they think Arden did. You have too much integrity and honor to ever get involved with someone who deserves a spot on the most wanted list, Kane."

"So you didn't call the police?" Kane asked, glancing at the officer.

"Good gravy train! Why would we do something like that?" Jules exclaimed. "We trust you to know what's going on and to find a way out of it."

"That's not going to happen if we stay here much longer," Silas grumbled.

"Right. Logic dictates that if there's one police officer here, more are probably coming," Henry said. "You three go do what you need to do. We'll take care of Chuck."

"If he realizes we were here, you both could be in trouble," Kane warned.

"He's still out cold. We'll wake him up after you leave and tell him we heard a noise and went out to investigate. That we found him unconscious in the snow, poor man, and dragged him into the house out of the cold."

"He's going to ask about me," Kane said.

"We haven't seen you and have no idea what's going on." Jules pulled a bag of corn from the freezer.

"And that last part, of course, is true. We're clueless. When it's all over, I hope you'll fill us in." Henry took Arden's arm and walked her through the mudroom to the back door.

"I need to get Sebastian," she said, pulling away and not promising anything. She wasn't sure if she'd be able to tell the Walkers what was going on. She wasn't even sure if she'd see them again.

"The cat? Is he really going to want to ride in the car with that dog?" Henry asked.

"He's not going to have a choice."

"He will if you leave him with us. We'll take good care of him until you return," Henry offered.

"I can't. He'll think I abandoned him." Arden turned, ready to get Sebastian, but Kane blocked her path.

His expression was grim. "Chuck is starting to come to. We need to move out."

"I *need* to get Sebastian."

"I know you love the cat, Arden, but you're going to have to make a decision here." He opened the back door, letting cold air blow into the mudroom. "You walk back into the kitchen, and you're going to be seen by a guy who is going to be happy to tell every police officer in the area that you were here. There'll be blockades up from here to Boston, and we'll be fortunate to make it onto the interstate before we're caught."

He was right.

She knew it.

She still didn't want to leave Sebastian.

"Arden?" He touched her cheek, and she found herself looking into his eyes. Found herself thinking about all the ways he and his parents could be hurt if she was caught.

She loved Sebastian, but he'd be fine without her for a few days.

"Okay."

He smiled, tucking a strand of hair behind her ear, his fingers lingering for a moment. She could still feel their warmth after he stepped away, after they walked outside, after they climbed into the back seat of Silas's vehicle.

That should have bothered her.

It should have made her nervous. It should have set off alarms and warning bells, made her toss up walls and create boundaries.

Should have, but all it really did was make her wonder why she'd spent so much time with Randy when he'd never ever made her feel what Kane did.

"Where to?" Silas asked as he started the engine and pulled away from the house.

She hadn't thought about it. Not much. She'd been too busy thinking about decrypting the files, escaping GeoArray, outwitting the FBI.

Now, though, she'd accomplished her first goal. She knew what GeoArray planned. She also knew exactly what she needed to do to stop it.

"Boston," she answered. "We need to get into GeoArray's offices and take down its network before the system prototype is transferred in two days."

"No way." Kane didn't hesitate. He didn't think it through. He didn't need to. There was no way he was bringing Arden anywhere near GeoArray.

"Hear me out, Kane," she said calmly.

"I'm listening." But listening didn't mean he was going along with her plan.

"The day after tomorrow, GeoArray is getting

paid to deliver the weapons control system. Once that's leaked, our own weapons systems can be used against us and our allies. We need to take down GeoArray's network system to prevent that from happening."

"Then remotely log onto the network and take it down. You hacked in before, you can do it again."

"I can't. Once I took the files from their network, they knew it had been breached. They took their system off the net. It's completely inaccessible to anyone outside their facility."

"So we'll take the information to the FBI and let them handle it."

"They may not be able to get a search warrant quickly enough to give them time to stop this from going down," she argued. "Plus, we know Emory has the FBI's ear. Someone could tip him off. By the time they get into the GeoArray systems, the information could be out, and our national defense will be compromised."

"They'll move quickly. They'll have to. We take the evidence to Grayson, he'll know who to trust," Kane said grimly.

"Even then, the government doesn't always move quickly," Silas said. "I'm going to have to take Arden's side on this. We should move in now while there's still time. Take GeoArray by surprise."

"I disagree," Kane argued. "There has to be another way."

"There isn't. If I'd had time to leave a worm while I accessed their system, I could have wiped out their network. Unfortunately, their network monitoring system found me too quickly. There is absolutely no way to wipe out that system except from the inside. We go in, or we allow the country's entire defense system to be vulnerable."

"Then you tell us how to do it. Silas and I will go in. You call the shots via phone."

"Statistically speaking, there's more chance of a meteorite falling on GeoArray and taking out the system than there is of that plan succeeding."

"Ouch!" Silas said. "You don't have much confidence in us."

"I have plenty of confidence in you, but this will only succeed if we work together. If you go it alone, you'll be in enemy territory, talking to me over a phone, trying to do something it took years for me to learn. All I need you to do is get me in the building. I can do the rest."

She had a point.

Kane didn't want to admit it.

But they'd need to get in and get out quickly and silently. Stay under the radar. That would be hard to do while trying to communicate with someone on the outside.

"Fine. You win."

"I do?" She sounded shocked.

"Why are you surprised?"

"Because I haven't won a debate with you yet."

"There's a first for everything."

She smiled and leaned her head back against the seat, sighing.

"Tired?"

"No. Just enjoying the victory." She met his eyes, and he found himself smiling right back at her, because she was Arden. She loved cats and Christmas and her country. She was smart, quick-minded and honest as they come, and he liked that. He liked her, and he was starting to think he could feel a lot more than that if he let himself.

"No one should be claiming victory yet. Not until we've gotten in and out of GeoArray without getting ourselves killed," Silas muttered, merging onto the highway.

"You have a point," Arden agreed. "We can't just waltz in the front door and demand access to the server."

"Once we get to Boston, we may be able to track down the blueprint of the building and get an idea of what access we can use." Kane could think of a dozen areas that were probably weak in security: upper level windows, ventilation systems, delivery bays.

One of his company's specialties was identifying physical security weaknesses for clients and shoring them up. Most companies didn't bother hiring outside experts, though. Most thought their security could never be breached.

Most were wrong.

"We can probably do that now." Arden tugged at the strap of her backpack. Kane hadn't removed it when he'd gotten in Silas's SUV. He'd been in too much of a hurry to bother. "Hand me my laptop. I can take a look through city records and see what I can find. I'm sure there's a digital file of it somewhere."

He shrugged out of the pack and pulled out the computer.

Seconds later, she had it open, booted up and connected to the internet through her wireless network card.

They bounced over a rut in the road, but she didn't seem to notice. She also didn't seem to notice the landscape changing, the lights of the city shining in the distance, time passing. She was completely engrossed in what she was doing, and he let her be.

He had things to do, too. Plans to make.

They'd go into GeoArray together. They'd come out together.

That was the goal, but anything could happen.

The company had money, resources and a lot to lose if they were unable to deliver the information in those files. If something were to happen that prevented Arden from taking down the server, GeoArray would successfully pass on information vital to national security.

Kane couldn't let that happen. He couldn't take a chance that they'd fail and that the secrets they'd discovered would be kept. And of course he wanted to clear Arden's name. Give her life back to her and have her home in time to enjoy Christmas with her family.

He had every reason to succeed and he had no intention of dying before he completed the mission. He had no intention of allowing Arden or Silas to die, either. But he'd be foolish if he let them walk into GeoArray without a backup plan.

He couldn't call in the local authorities. They'd stop the operation before it began. He couldn't contact the FBI for the same reason.

He *could* contact Grayson, though. But not yet. Not until right before they went in. He'd need to convince Arden to email him the files, too. That was the only way to be sure the information would get into the hands of someone who would know what to do with it if the mission went south.

THIRTEEN

They reached Boston in less than two hours. Gray morning light filtered through thick clouds and between tall buildings as they crawled through rush hour traffic.

Arden had spent every minute of the drive searching the internet for the blueprints of Geo-Array's building. She'd finally hacked into City Hall's database and was searching through a disorganized mess of file folders.

Her eyes were gritty with fatigue, her mind numb. She'd been on the go for days, running on adrenaline and not much else. She couldn't remember the last time she'd closed her eyes. Aside from the breakfast sandwich Kane had made her, she couldn't recall eating anything in the past forty-eight hours.

Yeah. She was a mess.

A mess who had to take down GeoArray's server system in a few hours. She scowled, scrolling through the City Hall files. Her neck felt stiff from too many hours hunched over the computer, and she rubbed the knotted muscles.

"It's got to be here," she muttered, annoyed with the amount of time the search was taking. Usually, she was fast. Then again, usually she wasn't working on no sleep.

"Why don't you take a break, Arden?" Kane asked, turning in his seat to look at her. She looked up, met his warm brown eyes and for a moment was lost in the depth of them. "Arden?" he prodded, and she finally registered the question. She blinked back the exhaustion.

"I've almost got it."

"I'm pretty certain you said that thirty minutes ago," Silas said.

"Studies show that optimists live longer, healthier lives," she responded.

"They also show that people who go into enemy territory blind die." Silas pulled into a public parking garage, grabbed a ticket from the kiosk and tucked it into the glove compartment.

"Aren't you just a stream of warm sunshine on a dreary winter day?"

Kane laughed.

"She's got you pegged, Silas," he said.

"I'm a realist," Silas muttered. "There's nothing wrong with that. I'm thinking we ditch the floor plan idea and do some covert reconnaissance. One of us can do a perimeter search of the building. We might be able to locate an access point that way."

"Just give me another minute," Arden said. She

scrolled through the files on another page, and her heart jumped when she finally found Geo-Array's name.

She clicked the file, smiling as the blueprint popped up on the screen.

"Got it!" she nearly shouted.

"Can I take a look?" Kane reached through the center console, pulled the computer from her lap. He studied the blueprint for several minutes, and she studied him.

She didn't mean to.

It just happened.

He was looking at the computer. She was looking at him.

He had a tiny scar above his left eyebrow and a larger one at the corner of his mouth. Both were faded white with time. Next thing she knew, she was noticing the thin white line that ran across the top of his right hand and the deep purplish mark on the side of his neck near his hairline.

He turned in his seat, caught her staring, and she was suddenly looking into his handsome face, his dark eyes. "Everything okay?" he asked.

She nodded, her cheeks hot. "Fine. I'm just tired. A habitual sleep pattern of seven to eight hours a night is thought to be best for peak cognitive performance. Of course, the amount can vary based on an individual's basal sleep need and sleep debt, as well as age. There's also a small percent of people that are their best with only six hours of sleep. It's been scientifically proven. When they exposed rats to high levels of stress and little sleep, they found they were less able to perform tasks."

"That's an interesting data point," he said without rolling his eyes, laughing or otherwise treating her like she was an idiot. She wasn't used to that. Aside from her family and Juniper, there weren't many people who didn't at least smirk when she went off on one of her tangents.

"It's just some silly trivia that I probably read a dozen years ago," she murmured.

"It's very relevant to our current situation," he corrected. "And being exhausted when we go into GeoArray tonight isn't a good idea. How about you try to rest for a while?"

"I'd rather take a walk and scope out GeoArray's headquarters. I'd like to take a look at the building. See how much security they actually have."

"No," he said.

"We could at least drive past. We certainly can't just sit here. We'll draw attention to ourselves. Plus, it's a waste of time."

"It's a public garage. And not all of us are going to be sitting here." Kane handed the computer back.

"What's that supposed to mean?"

"I'm going to survey GeoArray. You and Silas are staying here."

"What! When was this decided?" Not while she was around to have some input. That much was certain.

"Now," he responded.

"Well, you're going to have to undecide it, because I'm not sitting in this car—"

"Sleeping would be a better idea."

"I'm not sitting, sleeping or staying in this car while you're doing reconnaissance."

"Sure you are," Silas said, opening his door and getting out of the SUV. "We're too close to Geo-Array for you to be wandering around. Its people have been looking for you for weeks. You think they're not going to recognize you if you show up on one of their exterior security cameras?"

"They may be circulating Kane's picture by now, too. We know they've connected him to the plane."

"I'm pretty good at being unobtrusive." Kane got out of the SUV, too.

"By pretty good, he means exceptional." Silas closed his door. Kane did the same.

And Arden was suddenly sitting in the SUV with nothing but a dog for a companion. She couldn't make out their conversation, their voices muffled by the closed windows. Admittedly, Kane was probably the best qualified to scout the facility, but that didn't mean she didn't have thoughts to contribute to the plan of action.

She reached for the door handle, freezing when the dog let out a quick, sharp bark.

"Calm down, Cujo," she said. "I just want to get out and stretch my legs for a minute."

The dog barked again, and Kane's door opened. He leaned into the SUV, looking her straight in the eye. "You're supposed to be resting, Arden."

"I just wanted to stretch my legs for a minute." *And hear whatever plans you and Silas were making without me*, she added silently.

"There'll be time for that tonight. Right now, please try to sleep. Assuming we get in undetected, we'll need you to be at the peak of your cognitive ability," he said, throwing her words back at her.

"I guess a little shut-eye couldn't hurt," she grumbled. "Do you think you'll be long?"

"I'm not sure. But you can rest easy. Silas and Dutch will stay with you until I get back."

"How long should we wait before we come looking for you?"

"Forever," he said.

"That's a long time, Kane."

"My point is, I don't want you to come looking. I'll be back by lunch time. If I'm not, Silas will know what to do."

Be careful, she wanted to say, but he closed the door, stood for a few more minutes talking to Silas, and then walked away, sauntering along like he had all the time in the world.

* * *

Getting close to GeoArray wasn't going to be complicated. Kane had been in more difficult circumstances on more dangerous missions. Compared to those, doing a little recon on a traitorous tech company would be a piece of cake.

The complicated part would come later, after the sun went down. He'd studied the blueprints; he knew that GeoArray had an intricate ventilation system. The vent cover should be on the western side of the building at—or very close to—ground level. He needed to make certain it was there. Blueprints were great, but they weren't always accurate.

He jogged down three flights of stairs, exited the stairwell and walked into the lowest level of the parking garage.

Although visible from the public parking garage, GeoArray was across a small side street. Kane walked outside, following the sidewalk to the nearest crosswalk. A crowd of people waited there, most of them on phones, several carrying briefcases. Normal people going about their normal business. None of them had any idea how close the country was to disaster. The information GeoArray planned to release threatened the well-being of the entire nation.

Greed.

It made smart people do evil things.

GeoArray towered over the older buildings that

stood nearby. Modern and edgy with sleek lines and reflective windows, the place was huge—a discordant note in an otherwise quaint section of the city. They were close to the harbor here, the glint of water just visible to the east. Lots of people. Lots of activity. That made it easy to blend in.

The light changed, and the crowd swarmed across the street. Adults. Kids. Families. Like DC, Philadelphia and Gettysburg, Boston had enough historical significance to bring crowds of sightseers all year round. He'd come here often as a child, traveling with his grandparents during his breaks from boarding school. Boston had been one of their favorite haunts, his grandfather's passion for history dictating their travel plans.

He frowned.

He didn't have time for introspection. He sure couldn't afford to be distracted.

He stepped onto to the sidewalk with the rest of the crowd, making sure he was in the center of the swarm. There were security cameras near Geo-Array's front door and several more at both corners of the building. He noted those and the guard who stood nonchalantly in front of the building. No firearm that Kane could see, but that didn't mean much.

If the blueprint was accurate, the vent was on the east side of the building, close to the back corner. An old cobblestone road led in that direction. He bypassed it, still walking with the crowd.

Heading into the alley from the main street would be a red flag to anyone watching. He turned the corner and walked around the city block, grabbing coffee and some pastries from one shop, then stopping at another to buy some cold-cut subs.

Normal things that a normal person walking near the harbor might do.

There was plenty of hustle and bustle, plenty of camera flashes and excited chatter. He followed a small group of tourists past GeoArray. No public entrance on this side, but there were several doors and plenty of security cameras.

The buildings to either side were commercial properties. He used that to his advantage, walking down the cobblestone alley and trying the door of an obviously closed souvenir shop.

He turned back, sipping coffee and scanning GeoArray's facility. There were several doors. Just like the blueprint had indicated. At the back corner, a vent sat flush against the brick wall.

He walked past as slowly as he dared. Phillips-head screws held it in place. There'd be a fan just beyond it. Easy enough to dismantle and remove with the right tools.

If he knew Silas, the guy would have an entire toolkit tucked away in the rental. He believed in being overly prepared. So did Kane.

He stepped out of the alley, merging with another small group. They were walking slowly, snapping photos of some of the older buildings and plaques that explained the history of the area. He took out his cell phone and did the same, taking a picture of the alley, zooming in on the vent and getting a picture of that. He snapped a photo of a small memorial marker that stood near the street and then turned to snap one of the back of GeoArray's building.

One of the doors was opening, and he lowered his phone, pretending to scroll through photos as two men stepped outside. One was a stranger— tall with black hair, wearing a suit that probably cost a small fortune. The other looked familiar— light brown hair cut short, expensive suit, thin build.

Randy Sumner.

Arden's ex.

The guy looked haggard, his cheeks gaunt, his eyes deeply shadowed. Whatever was going on, he didn't seem happy about it.

Kane gave himself just enough time to notice those things, and then he moved away, merging with another group milling around near a bus stop. He snapped a few pictures of the distant harbor and waited impatiently for Randy and his buddy to make a move. If they returned to the building, he'd go back to the SUV. If they left the area, he'd follow.

Either way, he had information he didn't have before.

Randy was in town.

As far as Kane knew, the guy was a consultant working out of GeoArray's DC office. If he'd flown into Boston, he must be feeling pressure to make sure the cyber exchange went off without a hitch.

The fact that GeoArray hadn't been able to find and dispatch Arden probably had her idiot ex sweating bullets. He knew what she was capable of, and he knew she wouldn't stop until she was forced to or until she achieved her goal.

The door opened again and a uniformed security officer stepped out. He was pushing a cart of luggage, and he didn't look happy about it.

"Where do you want it, Mr. Emory?" he snapped, loudly, rolling it toward the street.

Kane tensed at the name.

Emory and Randy together with a cart full of luggage all sounded like an escape waiting to happen. The two men made their way toward the curb.

"You called a cab?" Emory asked, glancing at his watch and frowning.

"Didn't you ask me to?"

"Don't get smart with me, Henderson," Emory growled. "I don't like it."

"Yes," the security guard ground out. "I called a cab."

"When it gets here, load everything in it and take it to the dock. The *Relentless Journey* is in its usual spot. Just leave the stuff in my cabin."

Emory slapped a wad of bills in the guy's hand. "That's for the extra effort. Come on, Randy. We've got a few things to discuss before I leave. Let's grab some coffee."

"What do you mean, leave?" Randy sputtered, his face flushed with displeasure.

As Emory and Randy approached the bus stop, Kane turned away, knowing he was staring and afraid he'd be noticed. He texted Silas to give him an update, his back still to the men as they moved past.

"We're both leaving, Randy. You go your way. I go mine. We knew it might come to this—especially with the elusive DeMarco girl still just out of reach."

Kane fell in step behind them as they passed, keeping within earshot of their conversation.

"The plan was to leave after the file transmission, if we couldn't find Arden and get the files back," Randy whispered. "Why are you packing up now?"

"My wife thinks I'm leaving on a business trip this morning. My girlfriend and I are going out for dinner and I'll likely stay on the yacht tonight. But I'll be ready to launch it tomorrow night in the event that you haven't retrieved those files. Not that I owe you an explanation. I've paid you plenty for your work. Or, should I say, for your girlfriend's work?"

Randy responded, but the words were lost as the men walked across the street.

Kane could have followed, but he'd heard enough. He was more interested in the yacht. If he could get on board, he might be able to figure out where Emory planned to go. Despite what the CEO had told Randy, Kane wondered if Emory planned to leave long before the exchange happened.

Not that the exchange would ever happen.

Not if Kane had anything to do with it.

He texted Silas again and let him know that he was heading to the docks. He tucked his cell phone away, finished the last of his coffee and headed toward the glittering water of the harbor.

FOURTEEN

Arden dreamed of Christmas.

Of family gathered in her parents' large home. Of good food and conversation, of laughter and off-key singing. She dreamed of hot cocoa topped with whipped cream, a fire glowing softly. Kane smiling at her from across the room. Cold wind whipping in from an open door. A dog barking.

A dog?

She opened her eyes, still groggy with sleep, and stared into Dutch's dark eyes. He leaned in so close, his nose touched her cheek and his hot doggy breath fanned her face.

"Are you going to eat me?" she asked.

"Kee-gur'-lah!" Silas commanded leaning into the open front door of the SUV and eyeing her dispassionately. Dutch immediately backed away. "I see you're awake."

"I see you're still grumpy."

Someone laughed.

No. Not someone. Kane. She could see him now, standing next to Silas, his hair covered by a black cap. He had a couple days' worth of stubble and a rugged outdoorsy look that made her wonder if he spent most of his life tromping through forests.

She was stretched out across the back seat of the SUV, her backpack under her head. Hcr laptop was still open and sitting on the floor, the battery charging in the SUV's power outlet. She'd spent a couple of hours prepping for the night mission and waiting for Kane. She wasn't sure when she'd dozed off, but it hadn't been dark.

Now it was.

Which had to mean that it was almost time.

She sat up too quickly, saw a million tiny stars dancing in front of her eyes as she opened the door. Her foot caught on Kane's duffel, and she nearly took a header on the cement.

She would have if Kane hadn't grabbed her arm, his fingers curving around her biceps. "Slow down, Arden. We've got time."

"It's dark," she pointed out. "And I'm ready."

"Not until you eat." He handed her a paper bag, his hand sliding from her upper arm to her wrist. "I brought back cold-cut subs. I thought you might be hungry."

"I'm starved, thank you." She began unwrapping the sub. "I'm going to love you forever for this, Kane," she said, just like she would have if he'd been one of her brothers.

Only he wasn't.

"We've moved on from like to love pretty quickly, Arden," he said, urging her back until her legs hit the SUV and she was sitting on the bench seat again.

"Just a figure of speech," she muttered. She removed the last of the wrapper from the sub and did everything in her power to *not* look in his eyes.

He was special, and he was trouble, and he was exactly the kind of guy she should *not* be saying things like "I'll love you forever" to.

Because she thought that she *could* do that.

She could also get her heart broken, her dreams crushed and all her silly little fantasies about forever dashed.

Again.

Only this time it would be worse, because this time, she'd be dreaming all those things about Kane. And he was so much more than Randy had ever been.

"I bought it so you could eat it," Kane said quietly. "Not stare at it like it's going to bite you."

She took a bite, swallowed. "This is so good."

"Eat up. We can't afford to have you distracted tonight." He crouched in front of her, brushing strands of hair from her cheek. "I know I don't need to tell you that I'm worried about what we might come up against in there. If I could take down the system myself, I'd leave you here and do it."

"I know what's riding on this. National security—"

"I'm worried about *you*, Arden. Which reminds me." Kane reached into a large pocket in his jacket. "I bought you dessert. It's gingerbread. It seemed appropriate. Since you like Christmas so much."

"You're kidding." She opened the small white bag, got a whiff of spicy ginger and sweet molasses. "You aren't kidding." She took a bite, savoring the lightly iced desert.

"A gun would have been more appropriate," Silas grumbled, polishing off the rest of his own sub.

"We've got those, and the security team at Geo-Array doesn't look armed," Kane responded. "Not that that means much."

"Did you see the ventilation shaft?" she asked, finishing off the gingerbread and brushing crumbs from her hands.

"I did," Kane acknowledged. "I also saw your ex and Marcus Emory. Emory has all of his things packed on a yacht. He's ready to leave the country once this deal goes through—unless he can find you and eliminate any threat of discovery."

"Is Randy going with him?"

"Emory may take his girlfriend. Randy's on his own. Both of them are going to be disappointed."

"When they don't get the payoff because they failed?"

"When the FBI takes them in before they have a chance to escape the country," Kane replied.

"That's definitely the best-case scenario," Arden agreed.

"Speaking of the FBI, I think we should fill Grayson in on what we've learned before we head into the facility."

"What! I thought we weren't going to get him involved in this until it's over? If he has knowledge that we plan to break into GeoArray's secure facility, he'll have a duty to report it."

"You've decrypted the files, Arden. We have all the proof we need. Marcus Emory is selling proprietary national secrets. If we weren't under time pressure, I'd turn this over to Grayson and let him and the FBI deal with GeoArray from this point forward."

"We already determined that could take too long."

"Right. We're going in. We're taking the system down. I'm planning on all three of us getting into that building and getting out of it," Kane responded. "But if that doesn't happen, someone has to know what's going on at GeoArray. I want you to send your brother the files before we leave. He won't see them until it's too late to stop us."

She knew what he was saying.

She understood his fear.

If they were captured and killed, GeoArray would get away with an act of espionage that would rival the Robert Hanssen case, which was the worst in FBI history.

She grabbed her laptop. "I'll send them to his work email. That way I can encrypt them with the FBI's encryption program. We can't take a chance of the files leaking out."

"You have access to the FBI's encryption program?" Silas asked.

"Yes, I've consulted for them before on special cases," she answered. She attached the files to an encrypted email and sent it to her brother. "Done."

"You're quick." Silas opened the SUV's hatchback. "Now, how about we get moving?" He tossed several things in her direction. Somehow she managed to catch them. Black gloves. A black cap like Kane was wearing.

She put them on, then set her computer on the seat, the screen glowing blue-white.

"Are you leaving Dutch?" she asked. The computer had to stay on. If the connection was disrupted, she'd have no way to reset it from inside the building and nowhere to send the command and control application once she removed it from the network.

"He'll stay back here," Silas said. *"Oh-wahn'-*

kah," he commanded, and the dog hopped into the cargo area of the vehicle.

"If he comes up here and steps on my computer, we're sunk. The connection needs to remain open so I have a safe place to send the files."

"Dutch will stay put. He'll also keep people away from the SUV." Silas shut the hatchback and rounded the side of the vehicle.

"Ready?" Kane asked, offering a hand to Arden.

She took it, allowing herself to be pulled from the vehicle. December wind blew through the parking garage as they made their way to the stairwell, and she wanted to press close to Kane, gather a little of his warmth.

She wasn't just cold.

She was scared.

There was no guarantee they'd be able to make it into GeoArray through the ventilation system. If they did, there was no guarantee that she could accomplish her task before they were discovered.

She didn't say what she was thinking.

For once, her nerves didn't cause a stream of words to spill out of her mouth. She was going through the steps she needed to take, mentally rehearsing the quickest, most efficient way to infect GeoArray's server with a worm that would disrupt system operations. She'd have to be careful to stay out of the system storage to preserve the network's integrity. If she did it right, there'd be no chance that anyone connected to the system could retrieve files from it until she restored the server and turned it over to the FBI.

They stepped out of the parking garage and stuck to the shadows as they approached the rear of the darkened GeoArray facility. Arden waited impatiently while Kane and Silas unscrewed the vent cover.

They set it against the brick wall, then disconnected and removed a fan that blocked the ventilation duct.

It took merely moments, but it felt like hours. Cold, moist air blew in from the harbor and seeped through Arden's layers of clothes. By the time the fan had been removed, she was cold to the bone, her teeth nearly chattering.

"This is going to be a problem," Silas said quietly, and she moved closer, eyeing the dark shaft that led into the building. It was small. She'd be able to fit, but there was no way either of the men would.

"Time for plan B," Kane said.

"Which is?" Arden asked.

"We try to get in one of the back doors."

"You're kidding, right?"

"No." He scowled. "I'm not kidding. There's no way Silas and I are getting in through this vent."

"You don't need to," she argued. "I can fit through, and I'm the only one who really needs to be in there."

"You're not going in alone."

"We could stand out here all night arguing," Silas said. "But that's not going to do us or the country much good."

"We're not arguing. We're switching gears." Kane started to walk away, but Arden grabbed his hand.

"We don't have time to switch gears. We don't have time to try something that might not work. This is our best chance, and I'm taking it."

"She's right, Kane," Silas agreed. "We try to get in one of those doors and set off an alarm, and that information will be out before anyone can stop Marcus Emory."

"No," Kane said again.

"You're letting your heart influence your head. That's a good way to get people killed," Silas responded.

Kane scowled. "What's your point?"

"If I were the one who could fit through there and take down that system, you'd let me go."

"You're a trained professional."

"Who can't fit through the shaft," Arden cut in. She needed to get moving before her nerves got the best of her. "I memorized the blueprints. I know the easiest path to the server room. It should take me forty minutes tops. If I'm in there longer, call the cavalry."

She released his hand and would have climbed into the shaft, but he touched her shoulder.

"Arden," he said quietly. She turned, looked into his gorgeous eyes. Even in the dim alley light, she could see his concern.

"Don't stop me, Kane, okay? This has to be done. I'm the only one who can do it."

He nodded. "You have forty minutes. Not a minute longer."

"Afraid I'll fall through the ventilation shaft and start spouting random facts about espionage and the death rates of spies?" she tried to joke.

He didn't even crack a smile. "I'm afraid of not getting a chance to see your Christmas sweater this year. It's one of my favorite parts of your family's Christmas celebration." His knuckles skimmed down the side of her cheek, and she felt the heat of his skin through the thin fabric of his gloves before he stepped away.

She wanted to tell him she'd be fine.

She wanted to explain facts and figures and statistics that proved it, but her mind was blank, her mouth dry with fear. She tried to smile and failed miserably, so she turned back to the vent.

"Take this." Silas handed her a multipurpose tool. "You'll need it to exit the vent."

"Right." She tucked it into the pocket of her pants, accepted a flashlight he held out to her and crawled into the ventilation shaft.

The floor and walls were coated with a grimy layer of dust. Not something that Arden was expecting. Then again, her only frame of reference came from watching movies where the heroine escaped through shiny, clean and very roomy ventilation shafts.

She was shimmying through what felt like a toddler-sized hole, elbows and legs kicking up a layer of dust that swirled in the beam of her flashlight. Although claustrophobia wasn't currently among the list of her idiosyncrasies, Arden could see how this situation could send her in that direction.

Stay focused.

Stay calm.

Think about the blueprint.

Two left turns. A right turn. Straight ahead until she reached the end of the shaft. The server room should be there.

Please, Lord. Let it be there.

If it wasn't, she'd be dropping down into an unknown room in an unknown part of the building. She'd have to find her way to the server room without being seen.

She took a deep, calming breath—as deep as she dared in the dusty shaft—and pressed on.

After a couple of difficult turns in the vent shaft, Arden's flashlight beam reflected on the vent cover at the other end. She flicked off her light and peered through the vent slats. The hum of the server fans were an audible and very blessed relief.

She was in the right place.

Now she just needed to get into the room without alerting security to her presence. Slipping the multipurpose tool from her pocket, she shoved it between the vent cover and the drywall and began to pry the cover away. It gave easily, and she barely managed to keep it from falling.

She slid it to the side, letting it rest against the wall as she half crawled, half fell into the room. Snapping on her flashlight, she scanned the server room for the local administrator terminals.

The computer was on, two screens flashing a screen saver with the lock-screen prompts. The last user had forgotten to log off.

Perfect. Now she wouldn't have to come up with a user name, just the password.

She committed the user name to memory and rebooted the system, placing her drive in one of the USB ports and the wireless internet connection in the other. The system came up, detecting both the wireless interface and the external drive.

Bingo.

Her custom password program was now tied in to the computer's start-up sequence. She needed to degrade the system but keep the evidence of GeoArray's crimes for the FBI. Not a complicated process, but it would take time.

Arden watched the progress bar scroll across the screen. Just like the watched pot that never boils, it seemed to take forever to upload the worm.

Once it was in, she ran the program and removed her external drive and network card. The worm would immediately affect every computer currently logged on the network without leaving any forensic traces behind. The beauty of it was that the shutdown would occur one system at a time, as users logged on, making it difficult to recognize the full scale of the problem until it was too late.

She smiled as the terminal went black.

Done. She glanced at her watch. With a little time to spare.

She pushed out of the chair and started back to the ventilation shaft. The sound of approaching voices stopped her in her tracks. No way was she going to make it into the shaft in time to shimmy out of reach of anyone who happened to walk in.

She moved the vent cover over the opening, then crawled between two server racks at the back of the room. She was hidden well enough if whoever it was just walked by.

The door opened. The light went on.

She held her breath, afraid even the slightest movement would give her away.

"I'm sure we can just reboot the server and the system will come right back online," a man said.

She knew the voice, and the breath she'd been holding threatened to spill out in a great gasping rush. She let it out slowly, her pulse racing.

Randy. Of course.

He must have been working in another area of

the building. Once he tried the admin workstation, he'd know they weren't dealing with an isolated computer.

A few frantic moments of fingers tapping on a keyboard, a soft hiss of frustration and she knew Randy had figured it out.

"What?" another man said.

"I think we've been hacked. The system's been compromised with a worm of some sort."

"What do you mean, hacked? I paid you to make sure this system was impenetrable. If we can't make the file transfer—"

"We'll make it. I uploaded a backup copy of the application to the stand-alone system on your yacht yesterday morning."

"The application wasn't complete yesterday. There've been dozens of man-hours of work on it since then, and it's all lost! If we don't meet that deadline—"

"We have bigger things to worry about. We were hacked. It had to be an inside job. I took the entire system off the web after we were hacked the first time. There's no way someone could have accessed it externally."

"Call security in here," the second man growled. "I want everyone in this building rounded up and brought to this room."

That was her cue to get out.

She was inches from the vent and out of view of the men. They were distracted, and she could either wait to be discovered, or she could try to make a run for it.

The fact that Randy had uploaded a backup copy of the application to an off-site, stand-alone system made the decision for her. She had to find the yacht and infect the system there. Otherwise, the rest of the work she'd done would be fruitless.

Randy was calling for security, his voice ringing through an intercom system. She used the noise to mask her movements as she shifted the vent cover and crawled into the hole.

Her feet scraped against the metal floor of the shaft as she tried to shimmy farther in, the noise echoing loudly.

Someone grabbed her ankle and tugged her backward with enough force to send her flying. She tumbled out of the vent, landing on the floor with a thud that stole her breath.

She bounded up, swinging wildly, connecting with a jaw, a nose, a soft abdomen.

She could have won the fight.

Would have won if it had just been her against Randy.

But the door flew open and two security guards rushed in. Four against her, but she still couldn't quit. She grabbed a chair, would have tossed it at the two guards, but a man stepped between her and them. Marcus Emory. She recognized him from photos posted on GeoArray's website.

"Enough!" he growled, yanking the chair from

her hands. "You're done, Arden. It's over. You lost. Take her to the harbor and throw her in," he said, striding to the door.

"If they do that—" her brain clicked along at hyperspeed, making connections so swiftly, her mouth could barely keep up "—you can kiss good-bye any chance you have of meeting your deadline."

"What are you talking about?" Emory swung back around, his gaze going from her to Randy. "What's she talking about?"

"Don't ask me. She's always talking. Mostly about nothing."

"Randy just told you that nearly two days' work has been lost. Currently destroyed by the worm I uploaded to the system here."

"Get rid of her," Emory spat.

"It will take more than a day to rebuild what I've destroyed. That means you'll miss tomorrow's scheduled transfer time," she continued as one of the security guards grabbed her arm. "I can re-store the data in an hour."

Emory turned again. "How?"

"This." She took the drive from her pocket. "I copied everything here. It's encrypted. It would take the best expert in the world months, if not years, to break my encryption." If it could be done at all.

"Take it," he said to Randy. "We'll go to the yacht, and you figure this mess out."

"I can't," Randy grumbled, his cheeks red with anger. "If she encrypted it with a custom program, there's no way I'm going to be able to get the information off of it before the deadline."

"Then I guess she comes with us. Cooperate and you might survive, Arden," Emory said. "Let's go." He grabbed her arm in a vicelike grip and dragged her into the hall.

She didn't bother fighting. She was getting exactly what she wanted. A trip to the yacht and to the server. Once she plugged the drive into the system, the worm would do what it was supposed to.

Randy and Emory weren't going to be happy when they realized it.

Hopefully, Kane would figure out that she was in trouble long before that happened. She had a really cool Christmas sweater to wear this year— a Christmas tree with real lights that flashed on and off with the push of a button. She'd hate for him to miss out on that. She'd hate to miss out on it herself.

But what she'd hate more than anything was dying knowing that she hadn't done what she'd intended.

People like Randy and Emory?

They should never ever win. And if she had it within her power to stop them, she had every intention of doing it.

* * *

They had her.

Kane knew it before his cell phone buzzed, knew it before he glanced at the text message that had come through.

There's a black car pulling up in front of the building. Looks like someone's going for a ride. Get the SUV.

Silas's message was brief and to the point.

Kane knew Silas, hidden in the shadows near the building's main entrance, had a clear view of the front door, but there was no way he'd heard what Kane had—the tinny voice echoing through the ventilation system, calling for security in the server room—but he knew trouble when he saw it. Silas had impeccable instincts.

So did Kane.

Yeah. They had her, and he wanted to run into the building to get her back. If he hadn't thought that would get them all killed, he would have.

A car meant they were taking her somewhere. A car meant there was still time. He hadn't heard a gunshot, and he didn't think Emory would be foolish enough to have someone killed in his building.

No. He'd want the dirty work done somewhere else.

Kane sprinted to the parking garage and jumped into the front seat of the SUV. He grabbed the keys and started the engine. He didn't turn on the lights, just sped down the ramp that led to the garage exit.

A dark Mercedes was pulling away from Geo-Array, its taillights glowing in the night as it headed east.

Seconds later, Silas emerged from the shadows and yanked open the passenger door. "They're heading to the harbor," he said as he climbed in.

"You're sure?"

"Arden was talking nonstop and loudly enough for anyone nearby to hear. She mentioned the harbor and a server and something about fixing what she'd broken."

"If there's a computer system on the yacht, that would make sense."

"Do you know where Emory is docked?"

"Yes." Kane had done a little research, talked to some people at the marina's fishing supply shop and gotten a pretty good idea. He hadn't been able to access the dock, though. It was guarded during the day, and he hadn't wanted to draw attention to himself by climbing the fence that surrounded it. "How many men were with Arden?"

"Four, including the driver," Silas answered. "At least one is a security guard."

Kane drove them toward the marina, keeping the taillights from the Mercedes at a safe distance to avoid drawing attention.

The thought of Arden being in the hands of

Marcus Emory made his blood run cold and he had to push back the worry. He'd flown critical extraction missions in the Middle East for the last seven years, a number of them under enemy fire. But none of those compared to this.

He'd promised Jace that he'd bring Arden home, but there was so much more to it now. There was something special about Arden, something that the world really needed—uninhibited joy and curiosity and intelligence.

She was uniquely beautiful inside and out, and he thought that maybe that was something *he* really needed. He was no longer that dumb kid. He'd spent years atoning for his mistakes. Perhaps it was time to embrace the possibility that God wanted more for him than a life of regret.

Up ahead, a set of modest iron gates were swinging closed, the Mercedes's taillights glowing from the other side of it.

The gate, which was open and guarded during business hours, was unmanned and closed at night, requiring an access code Kane didn't have. Instead, he found a meter on the street and parked. He was out of the vehicle and over the fence in seconds. Keeping to the shadows, he made his way across a sparsely treed patch of snow-covered lawn.

Whispered movement drew his attention. A glance over his shoulder registered the shadow of a dog in motion. Dutch scaled the fence in an impressive leap, his chain collar jingling as his paws touched the ground. Silas followed suit, landing almost silently. Joining Kane in the shadows, he motioned to the dog, who immediately heeled at his side.

"You said you know where the yacht is docked?" Silas asked. His voice was barely a whisper on the cold night air.

"This way." Kane jogged through the silent marina, passing several piers. He'd struck up a conversation earlier with a couple of retirees he'd met in the bait shop and discovered that the *Relentless Journey* was docked at Pier Six, the farthest from the gate. Ostentatiously extravagant, it had its fair share of detractors. Kane had spoken to more than one person who was less than impressed by both the yacht and its owner.

The guy might have friends. They apparently didn't hang around the harbor.

That had worked to Kane's advantage. The yacht was exactly where he'd expected it to be, the Mercedes parked on the street near the pier. Doors closed, lights off, it looked empty. The yacht was well lit, though. Shadowy figures moved along the foredeck.

Kane motioned for Silas to stay near the Mercedes and headed to the yacht, the soft lap of water against the hull drowning out his footsteps. A ladder to the aft of the vessel led to the foredeck. He climbed it quickly, taking out a guard who'd been smoking a cigarette near the life raft.

He dragged the guy to a dark corner, using tether lines to tie him up and a signal flag to gag him.

This was what he'd spent his military career doing: going in silently, taking out the enemy, making a way for the team to get in and take out weapons caches. Kane dragged the guy to the railing, used his own handcuffs to imprison him there. He grabbed a small Maglite from his cargo pocket and pointed it at the pier, clicking it on and off twice.

He didn't wait for an answering signal. Silas would board the vessel, search out the rest of the security team and take it out.

Kane was going to find Arden. He was going to get her off the yacht. He was going to stop Emory and Randy, and then he was going to make Arden's ex very, very sorry for underestimating the woman he'd supposedly loved.

FIFTEEN

Arden's nerves were taut, her composure held together by a thread. She had to believe that Kane and Silas knew where she was. She had to believe they were on the way to help. She had to trust that God was in this, that His way was perfect, that she'd get out of the situation and get back to her life. Otherwise, she might just give into temptation and start singing or talking or spouting useless facts.

That would do absolutely nothing except irritate Randy. She wouldn't mind that so much, except that she had to focus. What she needed to do—what she *would* do—was stay calm.

She was where she wanted to be, sitting in front of the stand-alone computer system, watching as Randy logged in as the administrator.

He was nervous. His face was ruddy and glossy with perspiration, his hands shaking as he typed. He looked like an understuffed scarecrow, his suit bagging around his skinny frame, his cheeks gaunt.

She almost felt sorry for him. *Almost.* If he

hadn't stolen government secrets and wasn't trying to pass them into enemy hands, maybe she'd have a little more sympathy for his plight.

As it was, she hoped he got every single thing that he deserved.

"How long is this going to take?" Emory asked. He picked up the portable drive that a security guard had taken from Arden's pocket when he'd frisked her. The rest of what she'd been carrying was spread out on a marble counter nearby—wireless connector, flashlight, screwdriver and prepaid cell phone.

The security team had disappeared. She thought one of the guards was standing on the other side of the closed door. She might be able to get past him, but she'd have to get past Randy and Emory first.

After she infected the system, she was going to be running for her life. Literally. There was no doubt in her mind Emory would kill her once he realized what she'd done.

"Be careful with that," Arden warned, her heart in her throat as she watched him flip the drive in the palm of his hand.

He met her eyes, his expression cold. "Do I look stupid?"

"Is that a rhetorical question?"

He slapped her—a quick vicious hit that left the taste of blood in her mouth.

"Hey!" Randy glanced their way. "Careful. If

you give her a concussion, she might not be able to access the files. Then what?"

"Sheesh," Arden said, refusing to let either man know how terrified she was. "Thanks for caring, Randy."

"It's nothing personal, Arden. I needed money. This was the best way to get it." He finished typing in his passcode and took the drive from Emory's hand.

"By selling out your country?" she asked, and he frowned.

"I'm not a traitor."

"You're not a thief, either, but somehow you used my encryption program to help him smuggle classified information to a recipient outside of GeoArray. The initial files that were sent were bad enough, but if the completed application falls in the wrong hands, our national defense systems will be in trouble."

"I didn't steal your program. We collaborated. It was ours."

"Right." She snorted, knowing that that would get a rise out of him. "We collaborated on a lot of things when we worked on the university's research team, but that program was not one of them." She wanted him irritated. Angry was even better. The less time he had to think, the better. She might despise him, but she couldn't deny his intelligence. If he weren't working from a place of fear, he'd have considered the fact that the drive he was holding was infected with the worm she'd used to take down GeoArray's system.

"Enough chitchat. I asked a question," Emory snapped. "How long will this take?"

"It depends on how intricate her encryption program is." Randy plugged the drive into the port, and Arden's heart skipped a dozen beats. She was *this* close to destroying everything these men were working toward.

Please, God, let this work, she prayed silently.

"Let her do it then," Emory said. "I want it done quickly, Ms. DeMarco."

"It will be." She tried to match his tone, use the same cold, hard inflections he had, but her voice was shaking. She was disgusted to see that her hands were shaking, too.

She knew what she had to do. Fear would not stop her.

Had Kane and Silas seen her taken? Were they trying to figure out a way to save her?

She typed in her passcode incorrectly, knowing how the program would react. It was her failsafe, her backup plan. If anyone tried to access the files without the code, the worm automatically uploaded to the system thirty seconds after the first failed entry. The only way to stop it was to enter the correct code.

She had no intention of doing that.

"What happened?" Randy asked, leaning in as the passcode prompt appeared again.

"Shaky hands," she lied, typing in another wrong code.

The server was on borrowed time. Unfortunately, Arden was pretty sure she was, too.

The upload box appeared, ticking off the seconds as the worm infiltrated the system.

"Is that it?" Emory asked, leaning close to the screen.

"I…think so," Randy responded, but she knew he was worried. Unlike Emory, he understood computers. He knew that her passcode should have opened a screen with file options that she could choose from. This upload was different. This was a one-way ticket to Randy's failure.

He met Arden's eyes, and she could see the anger there.

He'd been bested at his game.

He knew it.

The upload box filled, then the screen went black. Randy's quiet curse filled the sudden deafening silence. The system had shut down completely. No more soft hum of drive fans. Nothing but the harsh sound of Randy's frantic, furious breaths.

"What just happened?" Emory demanded.

"She compromised the system," Randy bit out. "She uploaded a worm and destroyed everything."

"Were you planning to die tonight?" Emory yelled, dragging Arden from the chair and throwing her against the wall. Every bit of air left her lungs at the impact, but she didn't have time to recover. He was on her again, screaming into her face, demanding she bring the program back up.

She'd been trained for this. Her brothers had made certain she could defend herself. She knew what to do. She just needed her body to cooperate with what her brain was demanding.

She slammed her head into his chin, the force of the blow knocking him backward. The door was just a few feet away, and she lunged for it, praying it wasn't locked, praying she'd make it out.

She turned the knob, yanking on it with so much force the door slammed into the wall, bouncing back as she darted through. The security guard was leaning against the far wall of the captain's quarters, his head down.

He looked up from his cell phone as she raced out, stunned confusion crossing his face.

One more door, and she'd be on the deck. From there, she could jump overboard if she had to.

"Don't just stand there," Emory yelled as he nearly flew out of the server room. "Stop her."

The security guard finally moved, darting toward her, grabbing a handful of her jacket as she raced toward the door.

She swung around, using the flat of her hand against his nose. He cursed and fell back, blood oozing from his nose.

She thought she heard footsteps outside the door, but she didn't have time to worry about it. She had the door open and was running, feet slipping on wet flooring as she raced toward the stairs.

She could see the sky through the stairwell opening. The stars sparkled against the blackness. She could feel the cold air wafting down, smell the briny scent of saltwater. All of it was there, clear and crisp and vivid. Freedom. Just a few more yards away.

An explosion rocked the yacht.

Or, maybe, it just rocked her.

She stumbled, falling onto the stairs. Pain stole every thought as blood spurted from a wound in her shoulder.

Shot. Her mind finally registered it, and she was up again. She dodged this time, weaving and ducking even though the stairs were a straight line up and a bullet could easily find her again.

Another gunshot came from the left, glass shattering as a porthole imploded. She wasn't sure who was shooting at her. She just knew she had to keep moving.

A dark figure appeared in front of her, blocking the sky and the cold. She planned to plow through him because she sure wasn't going to stop. No way was she going to die in the bowels of Emory's yacht.

She slammed into a hard body, felt an arm wrap around her waist. And she knew before she saw his face, before he spoke her name. She knew without even knowing how that it was Kane.

She'd been shot.

Kane could see the blood oozing from a wound in Arden's shoulder, and it infuriated him. Her face was leached of color. She clung to his arm and offered a smile that made his heart break into a million pieces.

"It's done. We stopped them," she said.

"It's not done until I get you off this boat."

He helped her up the stairs, keeping one hand on her waist and the other free. Silas had taken out the guard who'd shot Arden, but Emory and Randy were still on the loose. He doubted Randy had a weapon, but he thought Emory might be carrying. The guy didn't seem like someone who took chances. He also didn't seem like the kind of guy who'd be happy to lose out on millions of dollars.

Arden had destroyed the only possibility Emory had of getting the rest of the money. If nothing else, he would want revenge.

They made it onto the deck. The second guard was still trussed up and handcuffed to the railing, the rest of the area empty and silent.

That should have made Kane feel better, but something was off. The skin-crawling, hair-raising feeling of danger seeped through his pores.

"What's wrong?" Arden whispered as he hurried her across the deck.

"Can you make it down the ladder?" he asked.

"What's wrong?" she repeated.

"I want you off this boat," he responded. The soft clank of feet on metal rungs made his heart race.

Arden must have heard it, too. She lowered herself over the side of the deck, her feet scraping against the hull. Blood was still pouring from her shoulder, and he wanted to tell her to be careful, but she was already moving. She eased herself down one slow step at a time.

He scanned the deck, searching for the danger he knew was there. Metal vibrated somewhere above, and he eyed the bridge, certain someone was there. Pale moonlight filtered down from the clear winter sky. It splashed across the upper deck and silhouetted a man who was walking to the railing.

Not Silas. This guy was shorter, broader, louder. Emory.

He lifted his arm, a handgun glinting in the dim light.

Kane didn't hesitate. He didn't issue a warning. His Glock was out, and he was firing as Emory took aim at the ladder and Arden.

"Arden, watch out!" Kane shouted, his words lost in the explosion of gunfire.

His bullet hit its mark, knocking Emory backward.

Emory's shot pinged off the metal handrail.

Arden jerked back, releasing the rail. The muffled sound of her scream was followed by the soft splash of a body landing in the water.

Kane was up and over the railing before the sound faded away. He could see the telltale waves where she'd gone under, the rippling circle spreading into wide arcs that lapped against the hull of the boat.

He tucked his gun in its holster and jumped. Feet first just like he'd done during dozens of training exercises. Only this wasn't training. This was the real deal. If he couldn't find Arden, if she was unconscious, if the bullet had nicked a major artery, if any of a dozen things went wrong, she'd die.

He hit the water almost silently, sliding beneath the inky surface, eyes open in the salty water as he searched the blackness for Arden.

SIXTEEN

She came up gasping and choking, water in her nose and her throat and her lungs. Lights splashed on the surface of the harbor—blue and red flashes of color against the darkness. For a moment, she thought they were Christmas lights and that she'd somehow found her way home.

Except that she was sinking in the black and brackish water of the harbor, her body weighted down by her coat, ski pants and boots. She tried to tread water, but her left arm didn't seem to be functioning.

"FBI! Drop your weapons!" someone ordered.

Whoever it was couldn't be talking to her. She didn't have a weapon. She didn't have a life vest, either.

Which shouldn't have mattered. She was a good swimmer. She'd always loved the water. But the frigid temperature had stolen her energy, sapping her strength so effectively she slid under the water again.

Don't inhale, her sluggish brain screamed, but her body had other plans.

She sucked in a mouthful of water, probably would have sunk to the bottom of the harbor if something hadn't snagged the back of her coat. She was hauled up, and water spewed from her mouth as she gagged up half the ocean.

"It's okay," someone said. "You're okay."

Kane. Of course it was Kane.

He pulled her against his chest, one arm wrapped around her waist, the other paddling to keep them afloat.

"You're my hero," she tried to say. But she was coughing so hard, nothing came out except a horrible croak that sounded like the death knell of an ancient tuba.

"Throw me a life preserver," he called to someone. His voice was hoarse with what sounded an awful lot like fear.

"Are you all right?" she managed to ask.

"You're bleeding like a stuck pig."

"I'll be okay."

"You'd better be," he growled as a life preserver landed in the water beside them. He grabbed it with his free arm and tugged her even closer.

"Are they going to pull us up?" she asked, so cold that the words only barely formed through chattering teeth.

He must have heard. "No. The paramedics have a boat in the water."

"That explains it."

"What?"

"The Christmas lights," she slurred.

"Christmas lights?"

"On the water. I thought that's what they were." She sounded as confused as she felt. Nothing felt real. Not the water or the cold. Not the throbbing pain in her shoulder and chest.

She took a deep breath, trying to ground herself, but she was floating somewhere between here and there. This world and another one.

"Hey!" Kane said, his voice sharp with concern. "No closing your eyes."

"They're open." Only she couldn't see anything. So maybe they weren't.

"Arden!" he said again, and she did open her eyes. Realized they were still in the water, bright lights moving toward them.

"The boat's almost here," he said. "We'll have you home in front of your Christmas tree in no time."

A fiberglass water rescue boat pulled up alongside them. Kane cradled Arden tightly as they bobbed in the choppy wake of the boat. The pain in her shoulder was getting worse. Every bounce and jostle sent shooting pain through her chest and down her arm.

"Arden!" Kane barked, and she realized she'd closed her eyes again.

"They're open, okay?" she snapped. Or tried.

Nothing came out. Not a word or a sound, and she was floating again, the water tugging her out of Kane's arms and into the blackness.

She tried to grab his hand, but she felt paralyzed, leaden.

"Don't fight them, Arden. We've got to get you into the boat," he whispered in her ear, and she realized that she was still in his arms, clutching his coat with her right hand.

Two other men were beside her, a backboard between them.

"Ma'am, try to relax," one of them said, his face pale in the flashing light of the boat.

"Is she conscious?" a familiar voice called from the boat. She thought she must have closed her eyes and drifted off again. It sounded like Grayson.

"We're going to float you on your back," the man was saying. "And strap you onto the backboard so we can lift you onto the boat. It'll be easier if you let go of your friend."

She did what she was told mostly because she had no strength left to hold on.

"It's okay," Kane said again as if saying it could make it so.

Maybe it could, because she was suddenly on the backboard, floating above the water, cold air flowing across her nearly frozen skin.

She felt the backboard slide up on the boat's access ramp. Hands grabbed the board and pulled it into the boat.

"Hey, kid," Grayson said, his face suddenly in her space, his eyes filled with worry.

"Is this a dream?" she asked as he dropped a blanket over her.

"If it were, it would be a nightmare," he said grimly.

"So…you're really here."

"Yes."

"Where's Laney?"

"Still on bed rest. Aunt Rose is taking care of her until I get back."

"You should be with your wife. Go home to Laney," she tried to demand. The words came out so slurred even she wasn't sure what she'd been trying to say.

"She's losing a lot of blood," Grayson called, and someone shoved in next to him, kneeling beside Arden.

"Ma'am, I'm going to apply pressure to your shoulder. It may hurt a little."

"Logically speaking—" she began, but a finger pressed against her lips, sealing in whatever she was going to say.

"How about we save your logical assumptions for a time when you aren't attempting to bleed to death?" Kane asked grimly. She turned her head. He was right beside her, water dripping down his face, a blanket around his shoulders.

"You saved me," she said.

"Not yet," he responded. He looked…scared. Terrified, really, his gaze sharp, his expression hard.

"You did. Emory was trying to shoot me. I saw him on the bridge."

"Emory is dead," Grayson said bluntly. "And the Feds and local law enforcement agencies are going to want to know why. You're both going to have a lot of questions to answer once we get back to the dock."

"Once she's stabilized, you mean," Kane corrected. His fingers trembled as he brushed damp hair from Arden's cheek.

"It's going to be okay," she tried to reassure him.

"That's my line," he responded with a tender smile.

She wanted to return the smile. She wanted to tell him how thankful she was for what he'd done. She wanted to say a dozen things, but they were all lost as someone pressed against her shoulder.

Pain exploded through her chest, and she was gone again, floating in the black water of the harbor, reaching desperately for something to hold onto.

She was out cold.

No response at all as the EMT put pressure on her bloody shoulder. Kane had felt fear before, but never anything like this. Arden was still, lips blue from cold, her right arm hanging limply from the backboard. He lifted it, holding her hand and praying in a way he never had before, with a desperation he'd never felt before.

Please, God. Save her.

Her fingers twitched, and then she was squeezing his hand. Her eyes were open and she stared straight into his face.

"Don't let me go," she said. "If you do, I'll float away with the Christmas lights."

The words were the first clear, crisp ones she'd spoken.

"I won't let you go," he promised. The boat bumped against the pier as it docked.

Her eyes were already closed again, and he wasn't sure she'd heard.

He'd keep his promise anyway. Just like he kept his promise to Evan.

He could still remember every detail of that night. A lone figure silhouetted on the windy bluff. Evan. A half-empty bottle of vodka next to him. A gun in his lap. Waves crashed loudly on the rocks below. Evan lifted his head. Saw Kane. Pointed the gun at his own chest. There'd barely been time for Kane to scream his cousin's name.

Kane had spent years trying to forgive himself for not being able to save Lexi. And in the end, for failing to save Evan. He'd spent years reliving those moments, hearing Evan's harsh rasping breath, the last words of his dying cousin. "Tell Mom I'm sorry. Make sure she's okay. Promise me."

Kane had joined the military and kept that promise, anonymously sending money to Evan's mom. It was all he could do. It would never be enough.

He shoved the thoughts away, pushed the memories back where they belonged. The crew lifted Arden's backboard and carried her off the boat.

He didn't release her hand.

He wouldn't. Not until he was pried away from her, and even then, he planned to put up a fight.

The dock was a flurry of activity. Silas was talking to agents, Dutch at his feet. Randy stood a few feet away, handcuffed and haggard, talking rapidly.

Kane couldn't hear what he was saying, but he was certain it was a list of excuses that would take weeks for the FBI to sort through.

Grayson fell in step beside him, his voice clipped and tight.

"Agent Keller from the Boston Office is here."

"And?"

"He wants to speak to you."

"I told Arden I wasn't letting go of her. I'm not."

Grayson frowned, his gaze dropping to his sister. "I'll do damage control, then meet you at the hospital. She's going to need surgery. You let her out of your sight except for when they're working on her, and I will personally make sure you spend the next few days answering useless questions at headquarters."

"It's not nice to threaten people, Grayson," Arden said without opening her eyes.

"It's not nice to let people get shot, either," her brother replied.

"It wasn't his fault. He told me not to go in alone, but I had to." She finally opened her eyes. "Where's my laptop?"

"Still in Silas's SUV," Kane responded.

"I need it." She tried to sit up, but the harnesses held her in place.

"Stop," Kane cautioned. "You're going to hurt yourself."

"I'm already hurt."

"You'll make it worse. I'll have Silas grab the laptop. You rest. We've got things under control."

"Not if the FBI plugs the USB into their computers. It'll take down their system. Don't let them do that, Grayson. Just get the laptop to the hospital. I'll take care of everything from there. I need to get the files—"

"Kane is right," Grayson cut her off. "We'll handle things. You just get better."

"But—"

"Oxygen levels are dropping," a paramedic said, dropping an oxygen mask over her face. "You need to relax and stop talking, ma'am."

"Story of my life," Arden murmured. Her eyes

closed again, and her hand tightened around Kane's as if she thought he could keep her from drifting away.

He climbed onto the ambulance after they lifted her in, borrowed the paramedic's phone and texted Silas to bring the laptop to the hospital once the FBI cleared him to leave. There was more that needed to be done to assure national security. The entity that had paid to receive the files still needed to be revealed.

Kane wanted to care. He *did* care, but he was more concerned about Arden. Her vital signs were dropping, her breathing becoming shallower. By the time they reached the hospital, the EMTs were working silently and quickly, keeping pressure on the wound to slow the blood loss, increasing oxygen flow. He could feel their tension and his own.

The ambulance doors opened, and a team of doctors and nurses appeared. They were moving, shifting Arden to a gurney, wheeling her through the hall, and he still managed to hold onto her hand. It was limp now, no desperate grasping.

"She's lost too much blood," someone said. "We're going straight to surgery."

"Sir?" A man touched his shoulder. "You're going to have to let her go."

Probably, but he couldn't quite make himself release her hand.

They reached the double doors that led into the

surgical suite, and the same guy stepped in front of Kane, blocking his path.

"There's a waiting room to the left," he said quietly. "I'm Lucas Riggs. Head surgical nurse. I'll keep you updated on things, Mr.—?"

"Walker. Kane."

"We'll take good care of her, Kane," the nurse said, and then the gurney was moving again. Arden's hand slipped from Kane's as she was wheeled away.

Nearly two hours later, and she still wasn't out of surgery.

Kane eyed the waiting room clock and wondered how much longer it would be.

He'd already given his statement, had his firearm confiscated for evidence, given his statement again. He'd used the phone at the nurse's station to call both Jace and Silas, who'd been taken downtown for his statement.

Kane stopped by the large windows that looked out over the courtyard. A dusting of new snow covered the walkways. Icicle lights hung from the windows and doorframes. Arden would love that.

She'd love the snow. The lights. The Christmas carols playing over the intercom.

The doors opened and Grayson DeMarco walked in. His black hair was nearly the same color as Arden's, his blue eyes not nearly as soft and inviting.

"How is she?"

"Still in surgery."

"I'm going to see if I can find someone who knows what's going on." He turned back to the door.

"I've been to the front desk every fifteen minutes. No one's talking," Kane warned him, and Grayson swung back around.

"I don't like being helpless," he growled.

"Join the crowd."

"Since there's only two of us, there's not much of one. The hospital staff's extremely fortunate the snow has grounded my parents at the airport in Baltimore or my mom would take up permanent residence at the desk until someone gave her some answers."

"Maybe I should try that," Kane responded wryly.

Grayson walked to a coffeepot that sat on a nicked Formica counter and poured thick black coffee into a cup. "This stuff taste as bad as it looks?"

"Worse."

"A perfect end to a perfect day," he responded, taking a quick sip and grimacing. "You didn't lie."

"I usually don't."

"We've got men in GeoArray, a team of specialists that may or may not be able to undo what Arden did. I'm really hoping that the two of you have evidence that proves it was necessary to totally degrade a system used by the Department of Defense."

"We do."

"Good. I'm staking my reputation on that."

The door opened again. The nurse stepped inside the waiting room.

"Kane? She's out of surgery. I'll take you back now." His gaze cut to Grayson, sizing him up. "If you're FBI, you're going to have to wait. She's not up to answering questions."

"I'm her brother."

"Then you can come back. But no more than two people at a time in the recovery room."

Kane and Grayson followed him through the double doors down a pristine hallway to a small recovery room where Arden lay. She looked tiny, her body shrouded in blankets. A monitor measured her heart rate and blood pressure. Clear fluid dripped steadily into the IV line attached to her arm.

The doctor, still dressed in surgery scrubs, was making notes on a clipboard. He looked up as they entered the room.

"Are you Ms. DeMarco's relatives?" he asked, pushing his glasses up on his nose and slipping his pen in his pocket.

"Yes," they answered simultaneously.

"The surgery went well. We were able to use a plate and screws to rebuild the clavicle."

"Rebuild?" Kane asked. He pulled a chair over to the bed and sat.

"The bullet went through her humerus and traveled up into the shoulder, shattering her clavicle. She's very fortunate it missed the major arteries in the chest wall. She'll need eight to twelve weeks to recover fully." The doctor attached the chart to the clipboard at the end of Arden's bed. "We'll be monitoring her closely, but the prognosis is good."

"Thanks, doctor," Grayson said, shaking the man's hand.

Kane would have done the same, but the surgeon was already hurrying away.

"Arden?" Grayson said. He touched his sister's forehead. She shifted but didn't respond. "She looks terrible," he said.

"Thanks," she muttered without opening her eyes.

"Sorry, sis. I thought you were still out."

"I wish I were. I really, really do."

"Are you in a lot of pain?" Kane asked, and she finally opened her eyes.

"Is the opossum the only North American marsupial? Are the echidna and the platypus the only mammals that lay eggs?"

"I'll take that as a yes," he said, lifting her right hand and giving it a gentle squeeze.

"You know what would make me feel better?" she asked.

"Christmas?"

"No. Well, yes, but…my laptop. Where is it?"

"We can worry about the laptop later," Grayson said. He pulled a chair over to the other side of his sister's bed.

"We have a twenty-four-hour window of opportunity to catch the buyers. That's when the file transfer was scheduled. If we miss the opportunity, we may never catch the buyer." She was pallid but reached for the button on the bed railing, obviously trying to lever the bed up.

"Stop," Kane said, and she shook her head.

"I can't. There's too much riding on this."

"We've got a team working on it, Arden. All you need to do is work on healing," Grayson cut in.

"It is going to take your team too long. I designed the worm to stay out of the system storage and preserve forensic evidence that could be used in trial. They'll never be able to recover the server in time. I'm the only one that can do it."

She met Kane's eyes. "You know it's true, and you know I can't rest until I do this last thing."

He did.

He also knew that he cared as much about her health as he did anything else. She wouldn't rest. He knew that. She'd lie in bed, her mind working through the computer system even if the laptop wasn't in her hands.

He reached for the bedside phone, ignoring Grayson's scowl. "I'll call Silas for his ETA. Last time we spoke, he planned to return to the SUV from the FBI's Boston office."

"Thanks," she said. She smiled like she had on the yacht, and he knew. Suddenly and clearly. No questions. No angst. No second-guessing.

She was where he'd been heading all his life.

She was the home he'd been searching for.

Her smile? It was the thing that had been missing from his life, and if her brother hadn't been sitting right beside her, he'd have told her that.

Instead, he dialed Silas's number and waited impatiently for his friend to pick up. He knew Arden would never rest until she had her computer in hand. And she needed rest to heal.

SEVENTEEN

Arden's small hospital room was packed. Two FBI agents stood against the wall. Grayson and Kane were sitting near the bed, talking in hushed voices while Arden typed right-handed.

She'd been at it for two hours, and her entire body hurt. She wasn't quite sure where the pain was coming from. She only knew it was there and that she had to ignore it. This had to be done. No pain meds until it was. No sleeping.

No looking into Kane's beautiful dark eyes.

It took every ounce of concentration she could muster to focus on the complex algorithms scrolling across the screen in front of her.

Silas leaned against the wall next to the window, dressed in all black. The medical staff gave him a wide berth, some glancing uncomfortably at him, as they entered and exited the room.

A young nurse in colorful scrubs with rosy cheeks and a nametag identifying her as Lisa, with a heart over the *i*, fussed around the hospital bed, checking Arden's vital signs and the IV fluids.

With a thermometer under her tongue, Arden

was doing her best to ignore the woman and focus on the task. A feat made doubly difficult by the room full of people. Not to mention that the overly chipper nurse seemed more interested in stealing glances at Kane, Grayson and Silas than in recording Arden's temperature.

Arden found herself uncharacteristically annoyed by that.

She was used to women fawning all over the men in her life. Her four brothers commanded attention from the ladies wherever they went. Arden usually found humor in it. But somehow watching the nurse covertly glancing at Kane when she thought no one was looking was irritating.

Of course, she couldn't blame the woman— Kane's quiet confidence and strength filled a room when he entered. Truth be told, Arden had caught herself glancing at him as well, only to find Kane's warm brown eyes fixed on her from across the room.

She took a calming breath and tried to ignore the nurse while she made a few adjustments to the reparation program.

At Arden's insistence, Grayson had called the FBI's forensic specialist, Harriet Clemmons. Together, Arden and Harriet had been able to establish a connection for Arden to remote into the FBI's network from her laptop. Grayson had forwarded the decrypted files to Harriet earlier, but Arden had still needed to transmit all the research files she'd collected, along with the files she'd swiped tonight.

A quick look at the evidence was enough to convince Harriet that Marcus Emory had planned to sell government secrets.

The question remained, to whom?

Arden hoped the answer was somewhere on GeoArray's network, and she intended to help the FBI find it.

Advised of the contents of the decrypted files, Harriet had pulled some strings to get a warrant for Marcus Emory's personal system as well as GeoArray's networks. One of Harriet's techs had retrieved Arden's external drive from the hospital, then met Harriet and the FBI forensics team at GeoArray's headquarters.

Once the USB was plugged into the network and the override code entered, Arden was able to remotely access the system and launch her program to restore it. Arden had already restored the company's networks so the FBI could perform a thorough forensic investigation. She only had one more thing to do before turning the network over to the FBI—discover who was at the receiving end of the stolen files.

"Do you need anything?" the nurse asked sweetly as she removed the thermometer.

"Coffee and doughnuts might help," Arden answered wryly, her stomach rumbling. She'd only been allowed ice chips since she'd awakened.

"Unfortunately, a doughnut and coffee probably won't sit well on a post-operative stomach," the nurse responded. "But I'll see if I can scrounge something up for you that might hold you over."

"Thanks," Arden said absently, her attention on the computer again. She was almost there. She could feel it, the cyber trail she was following, leading her closer to the answer she was seeking.

She shifted uncomfortably, pain stabbing through her chest and shoulder and maybe her arm.

"You need to take a break, Arden," Kane said. He offered her the cup of ice that was sitting on a table beside the bed.

"I need to figure this out," she responded. She continued to type, scrolling through lines of code one after another. She followed the trail. Just like she always did. Minutes passed, and the nurse returned with chicken broth and Jell-O.

Arden didn't have time for either.

She'd found a signature she recognized, one she'd run across on the darknet when working a forensics investigation a few years ago. It was tied to Alexei Petrov, a Russian citizen and hacker for hire. She pinged his system, located the associated IP address for the file transfer and slipped out the backdoor. Hopefully undetected.

"It's done," she said, pushing the laptop away. She suddenly realized how quiet the room had become. Only Grayson and Kane remained, both of them working quietly on tablets.

"You found them?" Grayson asked.

"I found someone who is affiliated with the email account Emory was communicating with. I was able to trace the backdoor he'd set up to transfer the files. I sent his name and the IP address for the end system to Harriet. My guess is he's hired help, just like Randy. The FBI will have to take it from here to determine if it's a nation-state entity."

"You're amazing, sis," he said, pulling out his phone and sending a quick text.

"I'm also tired." Exhausted really. Her entire shoulder and chest throbbed with pain.

"I can see that," Grayson said, heading toward the door. "I need to make a few calls. I'll go to the lobby so I won't disturb you." He opened the door and looked back. "I won't be long. Kane, you've got watch."

"I'm on it." Kane affirmed.

Arden closed the laptop and leaned her head back on the pillows, shutting her eyes against the ceiling lights.

Cloth rustled next to her, but she didn't open her eyes. She wasn't sure she could. Warm fingers traced a path along her cheek, tucking strands of hair behind her ear.

"You didn't eat your soup or your Jell-O," Kane said, and she realized she *could* open her eyes.

And he was there. So close she could see the

tiny scar near his lip and the fine lines near the corners of his eyes. So close she could smell winter on his shirt.

"I'm saving room," she said.

"For what?"

"Christmas dinner," she replied, and he smiled. He moved the laptop onto the table and pulled the blankets up around her shoulders.

"That's a couple of weeks away."

"It's never too early to start planning."

"Probably not."

"Definitely not," she said. Her eyes drifted shut despite her best efforts to keep them open. Somehow, she still managed to speak, spewing out useless facts that she couldn't even blame on pain medication because she hadn't had any. "Studies show that the best Christmas bargains are found during the summer months. Clothes. Shoes. Books. People who buy early save themselves nearly forty percent."

"You know what else studies show?" he asked.

"What?" She opened her eyes, saw his gentle smile and smiled back.

"That patients who rest heal faster."

"I—"

"You don't want to miss Christmas dinner because you're in the hospital, do you?" He crossed the room and turned off the light.

"Are you going to be there?" she asked. The question spilled out before she could stop it.

"With bells on," he replied.

"I'd like to see that," she murmured. Her eyes closed again, the dark room and soft beep of machines lulling her into sweet velvety sleep.

The muted dawn light seeped in through the hospital blinds. The hospital was just beginning to wake, the silence of the evening interrupted by the sounds of rattling carts and the murmuring voices of doctors and nurses making their morning rounds.

Kane stretched and yawned. He debated whether he should go for a cup of hospital coffee or play it safe with a soda from the vending machine. After Arden had fallen asleep, he'd argued with Grayson over who would stay with her and who would find a hotel for the night. In the end, they'd flipped a coin for it and Kane had happily spent a less than comfortable night in the blue pleather recliner.

He glanced over at where Arden lay, a little banged up but safe. To his surprise, she was awake, dark shadows under her eyes, her face drawn.

She smiled, though, just like she always seemed to. "You're still here."

"Where else would I be?" He walked to the bed and lifted her hand. "How are you feeling?"

"Like I've been manhandled, shot and half drowned in the Atlantic Ocean."

"So, pretty good?" he joked, and she laughed, wincing a little at the effort.

"How about you don't be funny for a few days, okay? It hurts too much."

"Sorry." He brought her hand to his lips, kissing her knuckles. He watched as her cheeks went pink.

"What was that for?" she asked, but didn't pull away.

"Does it have to be for something?"

"Statistically speaking? Yes," she responded.

"Then let's call it practice."

"For what?"

"The Christmas party."

"You plan on kissing people's hands at the Christmas party?"

"No, but there'll be mistletoe there, and a stunning, brilliant, funny woman wearing a crazy Christmas sweater. I'm thinking that if I time it right, I just might steal a kiss." It wasn't something he'd planned to say. It wasn't something he'd even meant to say, but it felt right.

Her eyes widened, and she started talking, spewing facts faster than a wood chipper shot out chunks of wood.

"Who says you need mistletoe to steal a kiss? There are other traditions. Like kissing at the stroke of midnight on New Year's Eve, kissing beneath the harvest moon. Some people believe that if you stand on the peak of Mount—"

He stopped the words with his lips, kissing her gently and sweetly and with all the affection he had for her.

Her hand slid into his hair, and she pulled him closer. The beauty of the moment shivered through him and made him long for more of this and of her.

The door opened, and she jerked back, her eyes bright blue against her fair skin.

"Wow," she breathed.

"I can think of another word to describe it," Grayson said.

"How about you keep it to yourself?" Kane suggested.

"I think I will," Grayson agreed. He walked in the room, his face carefully masking his feelings, a cup of coffee in his hand.

"Sorry for interrupting your…moment. I thought you might need some coffee after a night on that chair." He looked from Kane to Arden and back to Kane again.

"We weren't having a moment," Arden began, her cheeks pink.

"Yes," Kane interrupted. "We were."

"See?" Grayson kissed Arden's cheek. "You were. Which was obvious."

He handed the coffee to Kane. "I just want to know if I need to punch him for taking advantage of my sister or congratulate him for seeing how special she is."

"There's no need to throw any punches, Gray," Arden said, shaking her head.

"Then congratulations, man. I guess I'll be keeping my fists to myself...for now."

Arden rolled her eyes. "How about we change the subject to something more interesting."

"Personally, I find you very interesting," Kane said, just to see her blush again.

She didn't disappoint. "I mean the case. Have you heard from Harriet yet, Grayson?"

"She called this morning. They identified the buyer—it's classified, so all I can tell you is that it's a nation-state entity. We're teaming with the CIA to catch them."

"What about Randy?"

"He was transferred to Massachusetts Correctional Facility early this morning. That little weasel is being held without bond—Harry and her crew found enough evidence to try him as an accessory to espionage."

"What about the deaths of Juniper's husband, Dale, and his boss?"

"The team's still building their case. It could be a while. I'll push a little harder. Just to make sure they keep digging. But I feel confident—" Whatever Grayson was going to say next was cut off by his cell phone.

"Hang on, it's Mom. I asked her to let me know when her flight would get in this morning." He put the phone to his ear. "Hi, Mom...wait, slow down, what? Where are you?" His brows furrowed and he glanced at his watch. "Okay. I'm on my way. I'll call in some favors to get a private flight out and should be there in under two hours."

Grayson hung up, his usual calm demeanor slightly rattled. "Laney's having contractions. Mom and Aunt Rose are taking her to the hospital now. The airport's opened and Dad's on standby— he's hoping to get here later this morning."

"I knew you shouldn't have left Maryland," Arden said. "What if you miss the birth of your kids?"

Kane reached out and grabbed her hand, hating to see her so upset.

"Stop worrying and get some rest, kid." Grayson leaned down and kissed Arden's forehead, then ruffled her hair. "I'll see you in a few days." He turned to rush toward the door, then paused and looked at Kane. "Take care of her for us."

"I got this covered, Grayson."

"Make sure you call with updates," Arden yelled as the door shut behind Grayson.

"The flight to Maryland takes an hour, tops. He won't miss the birth," Kane assured her.

"I know," she sighed. "It's just Laney's not due for another three and a half weeks. She's probably scared and needs Gray to be there for her."

"He will be," Kane said with conviction. He prayed he was right. If Grayson missed the birth of his children, Arden would blame herself, even if it was misplaced blame. She genuinely wanted her family safe and happy. Would sacrifice everything for them. Just like he would sacrifice anything for her.

"But anything could happen," she worried. "Statistically speaking, preterm birth is the greatest contributor to—" He cut her off with a kiss, which ended too soon.

"What was that for?" she asked, her face flushed.

He smiled down at her, losing himself in her eyes. "That one was just for you."

EPILOGUE

Five thirty in the evening on Christmas, and Arden should have been giddy with happiness.

Bing Crosby crooned from the stereo system in the DeMarco home. The smell of ham and pecan pie filled the house. Arden breathed in the familiar smells of Christmas and tried on a smile. It felt as fake as the plastic mistletoe someone had hung above the living room doorway.

She could hear her mom and Juniper bustling around in the kitchen, their laughter and muted chatter barely lightening her mood. It should have made her ecstatic. It had been too long since she'd heard Juniper really laugh. In the days after Emory's death and Randy's arrest, Arden's friend had been looking increasingly drawn and tired. Juniper claimed it was morning sickness, but Arden suspected she was stressed over the ongoing investigation.

Evidence had quickly cast doubt on the circumstances of Dale's death, but her friend was still waiting for Dale's name to be fully cleared and justice to be served. Arden only hoped it would happen soon. The stress could not be good for Juniper or her unborn baby.

Arden rose from her father's favorite recliner and made her way to the large bay window. Her shoulder was still stiff, her arm aching dully as she moved. She'd refused to let it ruin her Christmas. She'd decorated cookies, just like always. She'd helped decorate the Christmas tree. She'd done dozens of things that should have put her in the holiday spirit.

Somehow, none of them had.

She sighed, squeezed in next to the colorfully decorated tree, and looked out into the yard and street. A light layer of snow covered the ground, its surface painted gold with the setting sun. It was beautiful, breathtaking, nearly perfect.

And she still felt glum.

With her arm still in a sling, and doctor's orders to take it easy for another three weeks, Arden had been relegated to light duty. Her mom had also given her the task of keeping Laney's Aunt Rose out of the kitchen while the Christmas meal was prepared.

That should have been easy enough, but Rose loved people, and she'd wanted nothing more than to be in the thick of things. Fortunately, Laney had handed Rose one of the twins. Rose was currently ensconced on the couch talking gibberish to little Aiden.

Laney held Flynn, and the two women sat side by side, sharing and reminiscing like they did every year. Arden could have joined in, but for once, she didn't feel like she had anything to say.

The men were in the family room playing a game of pool. Every now and then, one or the other would exclaim loudly at a particularly good or bad shot. Inevitably they'd argue that someone had cheated and there would be no clear winner.

Arden smiled at the predictability of it all. The family had expanded over the years, but the bonds between them were far from weakened.

Hearing a soft rustling near her feet, Arden looked down to find Sebastian under the tree. He was nestled between two immaculately wrapped Christmas presents and amusing himself by batting at a low-hanging bulb. She carefully knelt down and scooped him up with her right arm. He immediately snuggled his head up under her chin, his front legs wrapping around her neck. He purred loudly.

"I love you, too, buddy, but if you break another bulb Mom will kill me." She rubbed her face against the top of his head and thought about carrying him into her room and taking a nap. That didn't seem very festive, so she stayed put.

After her release from the hospital, and at Kane and Grayson's insistence, Arden had temporarily moved in with her parents. Her mom had been happy to have her home, of course, and Arden had enjoyed the preparations for the holiday, even if she hadn't been able to do much to help.

"Why so glum, doll?" Rose said. Arden glanced her way. Laney had disappeared and both babies were sleeping in their travel beds.

"I'm not glum," she said, her voice as bright and hard as a new penny.

"You think he ditched you, right?"

"Who?"

Rose laughed. "The man who was at the hospital every single day you were in it? The one who has driven you to almost every doctor's appointment you've attended? Kane Walker? Did he tell you he was coming?"

"He was supposed to be here a half hour ago," she responded. "He's not here. I'm not sure what your definition of ditching is, but that kind of seems like it to me."

"Half an hour, huh?" Rose patted her white curls and sighed. "That seems like a long time when you're waiting, but in the grand scheme of life, it's less than the blink of an eye."

"I know." Arden really did. Half an hour wasn't long. Anything could have happened to keep Kane from arriving on time. Her head knew that, but her heart was telling her something different. It was telling her she'd been fooled before.

"Of course you do. Just like you know he's

coming because he said he would. Some men are like that. They say what they mean and do what they say. When you find a guy like that, you really should hang on to him."

"I know that, too," she said, setting Sebastian down a few feet away from the Christmas tree.

"Then why are you letting your worries ruin your day?"

"I'm not." Much.

"I'm going to give you some unsolicited advice, Arden. Because I'm old and I can. Do you mind?"

Arden smiled, her first real smile of the evening. "You know I don't, Rose."

"Leave the past where it is. Enjoy the moments that are given to you and the people who are in those moments. Once they're gone, you can't get them back." She smiled. "Now, how's that for Christmas cheer?"

"I kind of liked it," Arden said. She leaned in and kissed Rose's soft cheek. "Thanks."

"If you want to thank me, go see if you can find some real mistletoe. That plastic crud has got to go." She waved at the glossy, fake-looking sprig.

"Are you planning to steal a midnight kiss underneath it?" Arden teased, and Rose grinned.

"Stranger things have happened. But not under plastic mistletoe."

"My mom left a box of Christmas greenery on the porch. Maybe there's some in there."

"No need for you to go outside, my dear. I was kidding. Fake mistletoe won't ruin this lovely holiday."

"I don't mind looking, Rose." The box had been sitting there for nearly a week, forgotten in the excitement of the twins coming home from the hospital. Arden had planned to drape the greenery around the porch railing and tack it to the windows. She'd also planned to put up the fresh green wreath with the pretty red bows that her mother had bought from the local Christmas tree farm.

No one had let her touch any of it. She was too weak, too delicate. She was still recovering. The list of reasons had been long, and Arden had been too tired to argue. But now the greenery was still in the box, and it seemed a shame to waste it.

She shoved her feet in boots but didn't bother with a coat. She wouldn't be outside for long.

She stepped onto the porch. Cold wind whistled beneath the eaves, and the air smelled like snow and evergreen and fresh apple pie.

She rifled through the box one-handed and pulled out a long rope of greenery. There were tiny Christmas lights woven through it, and she could picture the porch railing glowing colorfully once the sun went down.

She dragged the greenery from the box and walked down the porch stairs, the chilly winter evening filled with the quiet Christmas hush that she'd always loved so much. There—in that quiet expectancy—she'd always felt God's presence. There, more than anywhere else, she'd always felt at peace.

She wrapped the greenery around the railing, then added more to each of the balusters, humming Christmas carols as she went. Every bit of greenery that went up made her happier. Why not do what Rose had said? Why not enjoy the moments and the people in them?

It was Christmas of *this* year, and she was here to enjoy it.

"O holy night!" she began, belting out the familiar carol. "The stars are brightly shiiiiining—"

"If I'd realized you'd be singing, I would have gotten here sooner," Kane broke in.

She whirled around, saw him walking down the snowy sidewalk. He'd parked up the road, the driveway too filled with family cars for his SUV to fit. She could see the gleaming hood of his Chevy near the corner of the street. A man got out of the back passenger seat. She thought it must be Silas, but she was too busy focusing on Kane to pay much attention.

"You're here!" she said as she walked into his embrace. "Finally."

"Sorry I'm late. I had to take a quick trip to pick up a surprise." He kissed her forehead, shrugged out of his coat and dropped it around her shoulders. "I'm assuming you have a reason for being outside without a coat?"

"Just living in the moment," she responded.

"Could you have done that with a coat on?" he asked.

She smiled and took his hand, pulling him up the porch stairs. "I'm looking for mistletoe. Rose doesn't like the fake stuff my mom hung."

"I'm shocked," he said, tucking a strand of hair behind her ear and smiling.

"That she doesn't like plastic mistletoe?"

"That you don't want to know what the surprise is."

"Logic dictates that surprises are meant to be secrets that are revealed when the presenter is ready."

"What if I'm ready?" he asked. He put a hand on her good shoulder and turned her back to face the street.

Two men were walking toward her, a dog trotting along beside them. She recognized Silas and Dutch immediately. The other man was tall and broad-shouldered, his hair cut in a military style, his face partially covered by a thick layer of white gauze. He was using a walker, easing up the street like an old man, but he wasn't old. He looked about the same age as her brother…

"Jace?" she whispered, her heart recognizing him before her mind did.

"Jace!" She rushed down the stairs and met him on the walkway, her heart pounding in her chest. The last she and her family had heard, he was still in Germany trying to recover enough from surgery to make it home.

She stopped inches away from the walker, afraid to touch him. She wasn't sure where he was injured or how badly he hurt.

"Jace," she said for the third time, and he smiled, his eyes deeply shadowed.

"This is the first time I've ever known you to be speechless, kid," he said, his voice raspy and rough.

"I can't believe you're here. We thought you were still recovering."

"I am. I wanted to do it here." He released his hold on the walker and pulled her close. "I'm glad to see you're recovering, too."

"Wait until Mom and Dad see you! All they've done is worry about you and wonder when you're coming home." Arden kept her hand on his arm as he held onto the walker again. He was trembling, and she assumed it was from pain and fatigue, but he managed to shuffle along the snowy sidewalk. Silas walked closely behind him.

"You should have had them drop you off in front of the house," she said as they continued up the walkway.

"They tried. I refused. I won't get better letting everyone baby me."

"It's not babying. It's smarts." Silas spoke for the first time.

"We'll see if you say the same if you're ever

the one walking around with a metal cage holding you up." They made it to the steps and Arden hurried to open the front door.

Warmth drifted out. Voices. Someone asked about the open front door and the next thing she knew, her family was there, peering out, seeing Jace. The explosion of noise and joy was deafening, and she stepped back, making room for her parents and three other brothers.

Her father grabbed the walker, and her brothers flanked Jace. He made it up the five steps like an old man with achy bones, but he made it.

She let them move past, stepping farther back to give them more room. She bumped into Kane's familiar warmth.

"Are you happy?" he whispered in her ear.

"There are no words to describe how I feel right now," she responded, her eyes burning with something that was beyond happiness or joy. This was home and family and Christmas and love, every color and sound and scent vibrant and beautiful and heartrending.

"Speechless again?" he teased gently.

She turned in his arms, looking into his dark eyes. "Yes, but it's probably not something you should get used to."

He laughed and leaned down to press a quick kiss to her lips.

"Thanks for the warning." His gaze dropped from her face to her carefully chosen outfit. She'd spent hours deciding what to wear. She'd tried on a few dresses and even borrowed one of Laney's skirt. She'd put on blouses and cardigan sets and a dozen other things that just didn't feel right.

In the end, she'd opted for black jeans and the Christmas sweater she'd bought on clearance last January.

She tensed as Kane's gaze lingered on the fuzzy yarn Christmas tree, tiny blinking lights, pompom Christmas balls.

His gaze finally lifted, and he met her eyes with a sweet, tender smile that took her breath away. "Thank you," he said.

"For what?"

"Not disappointing me. You look exactly like Christmas should, Arden. And you are absolutely the most beautiful woman I have ever seen."

She probably should have responded, but she was speechless again. When he took her arm and walked her inside, she still wasn't sure what to say.

She'd always been the DeMarco boys' sister, the tough little girl who never backed down from a fight. She'd been the computer geek, the bookworm, the quirky woman who wore odd holiday sweaters, but she'd never ever been beautiful.

Until now.

Arden lit up the room. And not because of the flashing lights on her Christmas sweater. Her smile was bright and real and so beautiful it stole Kane's breath.

Every. Single. Time.

He watched as she moved around the room, hugging her mother and her father, sharing their joy in her brother's homecoming. There was no artifice with Arden. Everything she felt was painted in a million nuances on her stunning face.

She glanced his way, and her cheeks went pink, her eyes sparkling. She was what he'd been looking for since he was a kid. The port in the storm. The place to come home.

"Now is as good a time as any," Silas said quietly, catching Kane's eye.

"What are you talking about?"

"Ask her what you need to while her family is around. Make it a memory they all can share. That's what she loves most. Aside from you," Silas continued, his gaze turning to Arden.

"You're making a lot of assumptions, Si."

"Are any of them wrong?"

"No."

"So get to it. I'm starving, and if you start making your declarations of undying love at the dinner table, all the smarmy sweetness of it might kill my appetite."

Kane went.

Not because Silas had told him to, but because he'd been right—Arden was all about family and memories, tradition and home. She turned as he approached, her smile as bright and tremulous as the shimmering tinsel on the tree.

"We forgot something," he said, and she glanced around, frowning.

"We did?"

"The mistletoe?"

"It's okay. I think Rose has forgotten."

"Maybe, but I haven't." He took her hand, tugging her to the doorway where the shiny plastic mistletoe hung.

"But I'm thinking we shouldn't switch it out," he said. The room seemed to go quiet, the conversation fading as he looked into Arden's bright blue eyes.

"Why not?"

"Logically speaking," he began, and Arden grinned.

"Isn't that my line?"

"Logically speaking," he continued, pulling a small box from his pocket, "plastic mistletoe is better than the real stuff because it lasts forever. Like God and eternal life. Like love." He opened the box and showed her the antique ring he'd found in a little shop in DC.

"Kane—"

"It's just a promise. From me to you. That I will always be there when you need me. That when you're ready, there will be another ring and a wedding and all the things that go with forever." He took out the silver ring, a beautifully crafted dove in the center of a jeweled cross.

"It's…beautiful," she said. Her voice trembled, and he knew she felt what he did—the solemnness of the moment, the power of the bond they'd created together.

"Beautiful and unique. Like you. When I saw it, I knew it belonged on your finger. If you'll wear it."

"It's the only logical thing to do."

Someone laughed, but Kane was too busy looking into Arden's face. Too busy watching a tear slide down her cheek to wonder who it was.

"Don't cry," he said.

"Sometimes, there's just too much happiness to contain," she responded. She held out her right hand since her left arm was still in a sling. He slid the ring on her finger.

"I love you." He wiped the tear from her cheek. "Today and always."

"I love you, too," she replied.

"Then kiss already!" Aunt Rose crowed. "The mistletoe might be fake, but the love's sure not!"

Arden laughed, and Kane leaned down, capturing her joy with a kiss that promised everything he wanted to give her—love, family, happiness. Home. For now and for always.

* * * * *

If you loved this story,
don't miss Mary Ellen Porter's
first heart-stopping romance

INTO THIN AIR

Find this and other great reads at
www.LoveInspired.com

Dear Reader,

Off the Grid Christmas was especially fun to write because it gave me the opportunity to take a quirky, socially awkward genius and have her save the world and find true love in the process—and who doesn't like it when the underdog saves the day and gets the guy?

At its core, Arden and Kane's story is about embracing the things that make you different and understanding that it's those differences that make you distinctive in God's eyes. This doesn't mean you can't change or evolve; it simply means you should recognize that you have been made uniquely capable of fulfilling the purpose God has for your life.

It's also a story about faith and forgiveness. God offers forgiveness to those who seek it, yet—like Kane—some of us struggle with letting go of our mistakes. Forgiving is not about forgetting; it's simply about putting the past behind us and moving forward in God. We must fix our thoughts on what is good because dwelling on regrets drains us of the strength we need to become the person God wants us to be.

Mary Ellen

Get 2 Free Books,

Plus 2 Free Gifts—

just for trying the

Reader Service!

Love Inspired®

YES! Please send me 2 FREE Love Inspired® Romance novels and my 2 FREE mystery gifts (gifts are worth about $10 retail). After receiving them, if I don't wish to receive any more books, I can return the shipping statement marked "cancel." If I don't cancel, I will receive 6 brand-new novels every month and be billed just $5.24 for the regular-print edition or $5.74 each for the larger-print edition in the U.S., or $5.74 each for the regular-print edition or $6.24 each for the larger-print edition in Canada. That's a saving of at least 13% off the cover price. It's quite a bargain! Shipping and handling is just 50¢ per book in the U.S. and 75¢ per book in Canada.* I understand that accepting the 2 free books and gifts places me under no obligation to buy anything. I can always return a shipment and cancel at any time. The free books and gifts are mine to keep no matter what I decide.

Please check one:
- ☐ Love Inspired Romance Regular-Print (105/305 IDN GLWW)
- ☐ Love Inspired Romance Larger-Print (122/322 IDN GLWW)

Name	(PLEASE PRINT)

Address	Apt. #

City	State/Province	Zip/Postal Code

Signature (if under 18, a parent or guardian must sign)

Mail to the **Reader Service:**
IN U.S.A.: P.O. Box 1341, Buffalo, NY 14240-8531
IN CANADA: P.O. Box 603, Fort Erie, Ontario L2A 5X3

Want to try two free books from another line?
Call 1-800-873-8635 today or visit www.ReaderService.com.

*Terms and prices subject to change without notice. Prices do not include applicable taxes. Sales tax applicable in N.Y. Canadian residents will be charged applicable taxes. Offer not valid in Quebec. This offer is limited to one order per household. Books received may not be as shown. Not valid for current subscribers to Love Inspired Romance books. All orders subject to approval. Credit or debit balances in a customer's account(s) may be offset by any other outstanding balance owed by or to the customer. Please allow 4 to 6 weeks for delivery. Offer available while quantities last.

Your Privacy—The Reader Service is committed to protecting your privacy. Our Privacy Policy is available online at www.ReaderService.com or upon request from the Reader Service.

We make a portion of our mailing list available to reputable third parties that offer products we believe may interest you. If you prefer that we not exchange your name with third parties, or if you wish to clarify or modify your communication preferences, please visit us at www.ReaderService.com/consumerschoice or write to us at Reader Service Preference Service, P.O. Box 9062, Buffalo, NY 14240-9062. Include your complete name and address.

Get 2 Free Books,
Plus 2 Free Gifts—
just for trying the
Reader Service!

YES! Please send me 2 FREE Harlequin® Heartwarming™ Larger-Print novels and my 2 FREE mystery gifts (gifts worth about $10 retail). After receiving them, if I don't wish to receive any more books, I can return the shipping statement marked "cancel." If I don't cancel, I will receive 4 brand-new larger-print novels every month and be billed just $5.49 per book in the U.S. or $6.24 per book in Canada. That's a savings of at least 19% off the cover price. It's quite a bargain! Shipping and handling is just 50¢ per book in the U.S. and 75¢ per book in Canada.* I understand that accepting the 2 free books and gifts places me under no obligation to buy anything. I can always return a shipment and cancel at any time. The free books and gifts are mine to keep no matter what I decide.

161/361 IDN GLWT

Name	(PLEASE PRINT)	
Address		Apt. #
City	State/Prov.	Zip/Postal Code

Signature (if under 18, a parent or guardian must sign)

Mail to the **Reader Service:**
IN U.S.A.: P.O. Box 1341, Buffalo, NY 14240-8531
IN CANADA: P.O. Box 603, Fort Erie, Ontario L2A 5X3

Want to try two free books from another line?
Call 1-800-873-8635 today or visit www.ReaderService.com.

* Terms and prices subject to change without notice. Prices do not include applicable taxes. Sales tax applicable in N.Y. Canadian residents will be charged applicable taxes. Offer not valid in Quebec. This offer is limited to one order per household. Books received may not be as shown. Not valid for current subscribers to Harlequin Heartwarming Larger-Print books. All orders subject to approval. Credit or debit balances in a customer's account(s) may be offset by any other outstanding balance owed by or to the customer. Please allow 4 to 6 weeks for delivery. Offer available while quantities last.

Your Privacy—The Reader Service is committed to protecting your privacy. Our Privacy Policy is available online at www.ReaderService.com or upon request from the Reader Service.

We make a portion of our mailing list available to reputable third parties that offer products we believe may interest you. If you prefer that we not exchange your name with third parties, or if you wish to clarify or modify your communication preferences, please visit us at www.ReaderService.com/consumerschoice or write to us at Reader Service Preference Service, P.O. Box 9062, Buffalo, NY 14240-9062. Include your complete name and address.

HW17R